FOR A FEARLESS GRADE 6

BY: CATHERINE AUSTEN

JAMES LORIMER & COMPANY LTD., PUBLISHERS
TORONTO

James Lorimer & Company Ltd., Publishers acknowledges the support of the Ontario Arts Council. We acknowledge the financial support of the Government of Canada through the Canada Book Fund for our publishing activities. We acknowledge the support of the Canada Council for the Arts which last year invested $24.3 million in writing and publishing throughout Canada. We acknowledge the Government of Ontario through the Ontario Media Development Corporation's Ontario Book Initiative.

Cover Design: Meredith Bangay
Cover Image: iStockphoto

Library and Archives Canada Cataloguing in Publication

Austen, Catherine, 1965-, author
   28 tricks for a fearless grade 6 / Catherine Austen.

Issued in print and electronic formats.
ISBN 978-1-4594-0618-6 (bound).--ISBN 978-1-4594-0617-9 (pbk.).
--ISBN 978-1-4594-0619-3 (epub)

   I. Title. II. Title: Twenty-eight tricks for a fearless grade 6.

PS8601.U785T835 2014   jC813'.6   C2013-907635-2
C2013-907636-0

James Lorimer & Company Ltd., Publishers
317 Adelaide Street West,
Suite 1002
Toronto, ON, Canada
M5V 1P9
www.lorimer.ca

Distributed in the
United States by:
Orca Book Publishers
P.O. Box 468
Custer, WA USA
98240-0468

Printed and bound in Canada.
Manufactured by Friesens Corporation in Altona, Manitoba, Canada in
March 2014.
Job #201045

To my youngest son, Daimon, who inspired all the best parts of these characters. Thanks for helping with ideas, inventing good names, and reading my rough drafts.

September:

Dave cures Eric's fear of Dancing

#1:

Beware the back-to-school dance.

When the school bell rang at 3:15, the new grade six teacher at Lord Nelson Elementary jumped up and shouted, "Hallelujah!" He attacked the wall calendar with a black marker, destroying Friday, September 8th. "One week down, only thirty-five to go! Get moving, boys and girls!"

Mr. Papadakis had an old man's name, a young man's body, and an even younger man's mind. On the upside, he played in a punk rock band and knew that "5K8" was pronounced "skate." On the downside, he texted during class time and his favourite saying was "Sucks to be you."

In the back row of desks, Dave Davidson struggled to fit two binders, one lunch box, two library books, an agenda, a water bottle, a Frisbee, and a sweatshirt into his school bag. "I miss Ms. Samson," he sighed.

"Me too," Eric Leung said from the desk beside him, as he hurriedly slipped sixty-four coloured pencils into individual compartments of his art box.

Ms. Samson's friendly voice drifted out of the grade five classroom across the hall, saying, "Take your time, boys and girls. Make sure you have everything you need for the weekend."

At the front of their own classroom, Mr. Papadakis clapped and shouted, "Yo, just stuff your things in your packs and go."

Vanessa Raymond turned in her chair to face Dave and Eric. "You guys are holding up the whole class," she hissed.

"Yeah," Robbie Templeton grunted from the next seat. He scowled and huffed, creating a breeze for his fashionable bangs to flutter in. Whenever Vanessa said anything, Robbie said, "Yeah."

"Chop, chop, people! Out the door, please!" Mr. Papadakis shouted, bouncing on his toes. "Tell your parents my band is playing at the

Sugar Shack tonight. And don't leave without these!" He shoved an orange sheet of paper into each student's hand as they filed into the hallway.

"You're advertising your punk band to sixth graders?" exclaimed Taz Santos. He put his hands on his hips and puffed out his chest to better display his *No Bullies* T-shirt. Taz had passed the five-foot-two mark this month and he was determined to use his tall-guy powers to fight inappropriateness wherever it was found.

Mr. Papadakis waved the stack of papers and laughed. "What, this? No, this is some school thing. See you Monday!" he shouted, nudging them down the hall.

Dave had no room in his school bag — or his life — for another piece of paper. He read the page as he walked to the bus zone with Eric and Taz. "*Back-to-school dance?*" he exclaimed. "Why would we dance about being back in school?"

Claire Leblanc ran past him, waving her own

orange dance announcement. Her long, dark hair bounced off her shoulders and sparkled in the sunlight. She joined Vanessa and Robbie at the front of the bus line. The girls snapped their fingers and swung their hips, giggling and singing, while Robbie admired them. Claire looked over and caught Dave's eye. She waved and smiled sweetly. "A dance might not be so bad," he said.

Eric pointed to his red Converse sneakers and said, "These shoes don't dance."

Taz nodded. "School dances are hotbeds for bullying. The girls will wear high heels and treat us like babies. The grade eights will corner us in the washroom and steal our drink money. The parents will tell horror stories about sex and drugs in middle school. Why not just invite us to a public humiliation? Why even call it a dance?"

Nicolas Talwar rushed over just as the buses pulled in, with his backpack slung over one shoulder and his soccer cleats dangling from the strap. He grabbed Dave by both shoulders and pleaded, "Can your mom take us to the dance? Mine works on Fridays. Please say yes. Please!" He looked at the bus line and shouted, "Claire! Awesome dance moves!"

Dave tried to play it cool, but somehow he found himself nodding and shouting, "Yeah, yeah, you're really good."

"Dream on," Vanessa snapped.

"Yeah!" Robbie shouted.

Claire opened her mouth to speak, but Vanessa shoved her onto the bus before she could say a word.

Nicolas's house was three stops before Dave's, so by the time Dave settled into his room, Nicolas had already posted on the Lord Nelson Grade Six Facebook page, *So excited about the dance!* Underneath his status was a tiny picture of Claire and the comment, *Me too!*

Dave immediately called Eric. "You never know — a dance might be fun."

"Actually, you always know, and it won't be fun," Eric said.

"It might make us stand out from the crowd," Dave argued.

"You bet it would. Have you seen me dance?"

Dave had not seen Eric dance. But he'd seen hundreds of other people dance on the talent show he watched every week. And he'd seen himself dance in front of the mirror almost every single day of his life. "Let's just try it," he said.

"No way. I have an incubating fear of dances."

"Incubating?" Dave repeated. "What's it going to be when it hatches?"

"Maybe that's the wrong word," Eric admitted. "But I'm not going."

#2:

Girls like boys who like to dance.

Dave tried to do his homework at the kitchen table, but his eyes kept focusing on the dance announcement he'd stuck to the fridge. His old Burnese mountain dog, Maisy, nudged a wet snout into his hand. "Want to dance?" he asked her.

He coaxed Maisy to a standing position and placed her paws on his shoulders. She was not an eager partner. She flattened her ears and tucked her tail, deeply embarrassed to be dancing with a human. She jumped away at the first loud drum roll. Dave chased her through the house and out the back door, shouting, "But this is my favourite song!"

Their neighbour, a retired veterinarian, was

out trimming the hedge between their yards. "Don't chase your poor dog!" Dr. Walton shouted. "She's too old for that game. And you shouldn't dance with her, either, son. It puts too much pressure on her hind legs."

Dave wished that nosy Dr. Walton would let the hedge grow taller.

"Hey, honey," Dave's mother shouted from the vegetable garden. "Would you take Maisy for a walk, dear? Your brother has a stomach ache."

Dave's eighth-grade brother, Nelson, lounged on the hammock, sipping ginger ale. "Make sure to scoop her poop," he said with a sneer.

Dave hoped he wouldn't need to use any poop bags on his walk. Maisy was thirteen years old and he just never knew what he was in for.

Unfortunately, Maisy started sniffing in cir-

cles right at the edge of Claire's yard.

Claire hopped down the porch steps, smiling. "Hey guys!" She stopped short when she saw what the dog was doing. Or, at least, trying very hard to do. "Oh. Um. Hey. Are you going to the dance next Friday?"

"You bet," Dave said, smiling awkwardly, pretending that he and Claire were separated by something, *anything*, other than an old pooping dog. "I love to dance."

"Me too!"

Maisy kicked up some dirt and moseyed over to Claire, who petted the dog's head and whispered, "You're a good old girl, aren't you?"

Dave bent down and scooped the poop with his hands inside a flimsy plastic bag.

Claire wrinkled her nose. "Gross."

"Yup," Dave agreed.

"You want me to put that in the garbage?" she offered.

"Really?"

"Sure. Who wants to carry around a bag of poop?"

Dave shrugged. "Maybe Robbie Templeton?"

Claire giggled. "Don't be mean. See you tomorrow!"

Dave walked home with a jaunt in his step. A message from Eric awaited him: *My mom is supervising at the dance. She says I have to go. Help!*

Dave wrote back, *Have no fear.*

#3:

Friends don't let friends break their ankles.

"The dance will be fun," Dave said. He was in his basement with Eric on Sunday morning, supposedly doing homework, but actually watching YouTube videos of dancing dogs.

Eric sighed. "I hoped this wouldn't be necessary. Play some music."

Dave selected a dubstep tune, and Eric began to dance. His hips swivelled like they were possessed by a demonic Hula Hoop. His feet stomped without rhythm, his hands flew in all directions, and his face held a look of concentration that reminded Dave of Maisy during an especially difficult poop.

"It's painful to watch!" Dave cried, shutting off the music.

"I told you," Eric said. "I can't be seen dancing. It would destroy my reputation."

"You don't have a reputation," Dave reminded him. So far as he knew, he and his closest friends — Eric, Taz, and Nicolas — had always been solidly average in all departments: looks, academics, and popularity. He didn't think that counted as a reputation.

Eric frowned. He'd launched into grade six with three carefully cultivated fashion choices: red sneakers with black laces; black-and-red designer eyeglasses; and a red iPod in a black belt clip that would have looked awesome if electronics were allowed in school. Standing, sitting, or leaning against a wall, his look said, "Cool, artsy intelligence with a dash of Asian mystery." Dancing, his look said, "Just got off the bus from Nerdville."

"Maybe you could come to the dance and just sit around," Dave suggested.

"Have you met my mother?" Eric asked.

"She's Mrs. Participation. She'll drag me onto the dance floor in front of the whole school."

"Then you need a good excuse," Dave said. "Like a doctor's note. You can't dance if your ankle's sprained, right?"

"My ankle's not sprained."

"Not yet."

Eric frowned. "A sprain sounds serious."

Dave waved a hand in the air. "My mom sprained her ankle falling off a curb once. I don't think it's such a big deal. You could probably sprain yours on the way to the park."

The boys headed down the street. Eric dragged his feet, trying to stumble off the curb. "I think my fear of pain is stronger than my fear of dancing," he admitted. Dave stuck a foot in Eric's path, and Eric sprawled onto the road. "What did you do that for?" he cried.

"Did it work?" Dave asked. "Are you sprained?"

"No." Eric dusted himself off and added, "Just humiliated." He pointed to the park, where Vanessa sat on the swings with Claire, laughing at him.

"Now that I think about it," Dave said, "my mom was wearing high heels when she fell off the curb."

Eric scowled. "I will bite my ankle off before I let Vanessa Raymond see me wearing high heels." He bared his teeth to make his point. They were not very sharp. It would take hours of gnawing to bite off an ankle.

Dave smiled. "I know a kid who sprained his ankle jumping off a swing."

Eric stared at the empty swings beside the girls. "Really?"

"Really."

For the next twenty minutes, Dave sat next to Claire, chatting about music, dogs, and the weirdness of Mr. Papadakis. Eric sat next to Vanessa, ignoring her and jumping off the swing repeatedly, until Claire's sister called them home.

"That kid is so clumsy," Vanessa muttered as they walked away. "He can't even jump off a swing properly."

Eric stared at Dave accusingly.

"Now that I think about it," Dave said, "the kid who sprained his ankle might have  been wearing high heels when he jumped off the swing."

Eric cuffed him. "Got any better ideas?"

"I could sprain your ankle for you," Dave offered.

"What are friends for?" Eric twisted in his swing to face Dave. He raised his left foot in the air and said, "Do your best."

Dave held the ankle up near his face for close inspection.

"What are you doing?" Nicolas shouted from the street. He rolled into the park, hopped off his skateboard, flung off his helmet, and raced over to check out the bottom of Eric's shoe. He sniffed and said, "I don't see or smell anything."

Taz rolled into the park on his longboard moments later. He wore gloves, wrist guards, elbow pads, knee pads, and a helmet that made him look even taller than he was. "You go too fast, Nic," he said, slowing to a safe stop. "Falls are the number one cause of childhood accidents, you know."

"Not in my case," Eric muttered.

"Can you guys help me sprain Eric's ankle?" Dave asked.

"Sure!" Nicolas said.

"No way! That's bullying!" Taz said.

"But he wants us to," Dave explained.

Taz frowned. "Then it's some other mental health issue. Don't do it."

Dave's brother, Nelson, walked into the park with his only friend, Rick Munster, who was known to every student at Lord Nelson Elementary by his appropriate last name. Munster was huge, with long, brown hair he never combed and beady, black eyes he never blinked. "Looks like we found some longboards!" Nelson shouted, hopping onto Nicolas's abandoned board.

"Get off that!" Dave yelled.

Nelson grabbed Dave's head and twisted it like the cap of a jar. "Call me Lord!" he shouted. "Call me Lord Nelson!"

Munster blocked Dave's escape and laughed wickedly.

Taz looked at the hulking eighth graders, drew himself up to his full height, and said, "Leave us alone!"

"Unless you want to help bust Eric's ankle," Nicolas added.

Eric jumped to his feet. "Are you crazy? Don't involve *these* guys!"

The talk of violence attracted Nelson's attention. He let go of Dave and asked, "Are you trying to break your leg to get out of the dance?" Despite his Neanderthal tendencies, Nelson had an uncanny ability to read people's motives.

"No," Eric said. "That's not what's going on here at all."

"I'll help," Munster offered. "You'll never have to dance again."

Eric looked up at the biggest boy in their school and trembled.

Nelson laughed. "Don't wet your pants. We wouldn't waste our time. You'll have to bust your leg all by yourself."

#4:
You should research stupid things before doing them.

Eric tried to break his ankle all weekend long, stopping just short of high heels, but on Monday he arrived at school without a limp. "Maybe you could dogpile my leg," he asked his friends at recess.

"What do you think you're doing?" Mr. Papadakis shouted. "Get up!" It took the boys by surprise — Mr. P usually spent yard duty on his cell phone.

"Eric's trying to sprain his ankle to get out of the dance," Nicolas explained.

"Don't tell *him* that," Eric hissed.

Mr. P frowned. "Spraining requires a certain finesse. It's probably easier just to break it."

His phone rang and he walked away without another word.

"Do you think he has a real teaching degree?" Taz wondered.

Dave spotted Claire across the schoolyard. She was practising dance moves with Andrew McFadden, a slender red-haired boy who'd just switched to their school. Andrew hadn't said one word in class all last week, but there he was laughing, spinning, touching Claire's arms, and singing, "Five, six, seven, eight!"

Dave sighed. "We should work on a dance routine."

"You're insane," Eric told him.

Nicolas picked his nose and suggested, "We could play booger tag."

Thankfully, the bell rang.

Their class headed to the library, and Dave and Eric used the time to research the best way to sprain an ankle. "I'll go online while you look at books," Dave said, claiming the last free computer. Claire walked by, and Dave jumped to his feet. "I mean, you go online and I'll look for books."

Dave spotted Claire in the nature section

talking to Andrew. He slipped down the next aisle, peeking between the shelves.

"I wanted to see the new *Step Up* film," Andrew was saying, "but my little sister had her birthday party at the same time."

"You should see it this weekend," Claire said. "It's really good."

Vanessa tapped Dave on the shoulder and shouted, "Are you spying on people?"

He jumped and stuttered, "N-no! I'm looking for books on . . ." He grabbed a book at random from the shelf in front of his face. "On easy quilt patterns for baby blankets," he finished, reading out the title.

Vanessa peered into the next aisle. "Dave was spying on you, Claire!"

"I should get back to my research," Dave said, slinking away.

Vanessa laughed. "Happy quilting!"

Back at the computers, Eric was deep in online medical research. "Sprains take six weeks to heal," he announced. "And they leave your ankle suspectable to future injuries."

"Suspectable?" Dave repeated. "Like if someone steals my lunch money, I should interrogate your ankle?"

"Whatever it's called, it's not worth it," Eric said. "I need a faster-healing injury."

Dave shrugged. "My dad got food poisoning that only lasted two days."

Eric groaned. "Two days of food poisoning? That would ruin my whole weekend."

"Not if you got sick Wednesday night. You'd miss two days of school plus the dance , and be better by Saturday."

Eric frowned. "What do you actually know about food poisoning?"

Dave smiled. "You don't need to wear high heels to get it."

#5:

What goes around, comes around and ends up in the toilet.

Dave searched the snack drawer of his fridge while Eric peered over his shoulder. Dave pulled out a package of sliced ham that had expired in August. The edges of the meat were green. The package interior was slimy. It smelled like a dead thing in the sun.

"I'm not eating that," Eric said. He pulled out his camera and added, "But I might do a stop-time animation of its decay."

Dave nodded. "Take it home for that. But don't eat it — it might kill you. Let's try dairy products for a gentler poison. No one ever died from old yogourt, did they?" He checked the date on the yogourt. "This one's fresh." He checked the flavour. "Raspberry."

Eric licked his lips. "Let's fill my stomach before we empty it."

The boys ate yogourt and drew comics at the kitchen table.

Nelson barged in with Munster, laughing about kids in their class who were weaker than them. Nelson smacked Dave on the back of the head and bellowed, "What's to eat?"

"There's some ham on the counter with your name on it," Dave muttered.

"What was that?" Munster growled from behind Dave's chair.

"Nothing," Dave squeaked. He could never figure out how someone as large as Munster could move so silently.

Nelson moved things around in the fridge, grunting. He pulled out a tub of sour cream and lifted the lid. "Oh! Gross!" He waved it in front of Dave's face, shouting, "Eat!" Then he led Munster upstairs with a bag of nachos.

Dave peeked into the expired tub of sour cream. A disgusting blue mould bloomed inside it. He smiled and pushed the tub toward Eric. "Bon appétit."

Eric dipped in his spoon.

"Make sure you get  lots of mould," Dave said encouragingly.

Eric held up a scoop of thick sour cream topped with what appeared to be pond scum from the dinosaur age. He opened his mouth and brought the gooey spoon close to his lips.

Dave watched with wide eyes. "You can do it. Be brave."

Eric pushed the spoon inside his mouth and held it there with his jaw stretched wide. His eyes bulged. His hand trembled. He groaned from the back of his throat.

"Down the hatch," Dave whispered.

Eric shuddered. He accidentally smeared mouldy sour cream onto his teeth. "Aaaah!" he cried. He whipped the spoon out of his mouth, ran to the sink, and spat. He rinsed his mouth, spat again, wiped his teeth with paper towel, and rinsed once more. "I can't do it!" he cried.

"Never say never," Dave said.

"I didn't say never. I said can't."

"Never say can't." Dave toasted two slices of bread, peeled four strips of smoked meat, sliced a tomato, washed some lettuce, and built his friend a beautiful sandwich slathered in mouldy sour cream. "You won't taste a thing," he said.

Eric stared at the sandwich hopefully. It was rather handsome with the blue mould hidden inside it. "Maybe a little salt and pepper?" he asked.

Dave lifted the top toast, sprinkled salt and pepper, and closed it up again.

Eric was just working himself up to touch it when Nelson thumped down the stairs, shouting, "What smells so good? Did you make toast?" He spotted the sandwich and dashed over. "Is that smoked meat?"

"It's mine," Eric said, pulling the plate close. "You can't have it."

Nelson grabbed the plate and rushed upstairs with it. "Hey Munster, I made us a smoked meat sandwich!"

Dave and Eric stood at the bottom of the stairs, looking up in silence. Each of them wondered if they should stop what was about to happen, and each of them decided they'd much rather let it play out.

All they could hear from upstairs was Nelson's obnoxious music playing behind his closed door and occasional muffled laughter. They listened for five long minutes. Eventually Dave asked, "Want more yogourt?"

They sat at the table eating and drawing and listening closely. Eventually Eric said, "We should do our math homework."

They were on question six of ten when Nelson's bedroom door burst open. Music and the pounding of feet filled the air. Nelson thumped to his knees in the bathroom at the top of the stairs and vomited into the toilet. Once. Twice. Three times in a row.

Dave and Eric locked eyes across the kitchen table, their pencils paused above their workbooks.

As soon as the vomiting stopped in the bathroom, a painful groan rose above the music in Nelson's bedroom. That was followed by thumping, clanging, swearing, and a great deal of vomiting directly above the boys' heads.

Dave and Eric stared up at the ceiling,

grimacing. For a few seconds, all they heard was music. Then the vomiting noises erupted again — first in the bathroom, then in the bedroom, like a vile sort of musical round.

Eventually they heard the sounds of flushing, washing, and Nelson shouting, "Aw man, why'd you have to do that on my bed? The garbage can is right there!"

Dave and Eric laughed as quietly as they could and slapped a soft high-five.

"That was disgusting," Eric whispered. "I don't want to throw up. It's bad for your sarcophagus."

"Your sarcophagus?" Dave repeated. "If you're in a sarcophagus, throwing up is the least of your problems."

"All I mean is I need another plan," Eric said. "One that doesn't cause any pain or do any physical damage."

Dave smiled. "Let's turn you into a dancer."

"I said no pain," Eric repeated.

#6:
conquering fear is hard work.

"What is it you're afraid of?" Dave asked. "Being rejected? Being embarrassed? Waltzing with a girl who tries to kiss you? Falling on your face? What?"

"All those things," Eric said. "Now that you mention them. I was only scared of being a lousy dancer, but now you've added to my nightmare." He sighed and asked, "Do you really think some girl will try to kiss me?"

"We need a plan that covers bad dancing and the girl factor," Dave said.

"What's the girl factor, exactly?" Eric asked.

"Either they're all over you or they're nowhere near you."

"I don't mind if they're nowhere near me," Eric admitted.

"The best strategy is to dance with a group of friends." Dave grabbed the phone.

Nicolas answered on the first ring. "Of course I'm going. Your mom's driving me, isn't she?"

Dave rang up Taz for a conference call.

"I'll go as a show of support for Eric," Taz said. "But I don't expect to enjoy myself. Dances are very gender stereotyped."

"What does that even mean?" Eric asked.

"Girls always dance with other girls," Taz explained. "But if two boys dance together, kids make fun of them and grown-ups make them sit down."

"Not if they dance with a group," Dave said. "Let's work out a group routine tomorrow at lunch."

"I've got soccer tomorrow at lunch," Nicolas said.

"I've got leadership," Taz added.

"I've got a fear of dancing," Eric said.

#6: Conquering fear is hard work

"Then it's up to me to cure it," Dave said. "And I think I know how."

At lunch recess on Friday, Dave dragged Eric around the school grounds searching for Andrew McFadden. They found him teaching third graders how to make a cootie catcher out of construction paper. "Please teach Eric how to dance," Dave begged. "I know you can do it. I saw you teaching Claire."

"Actually, I'd rather make a cootie catcher," Eric said.

The new kid was no fool. "I'll do it if you guys come to *Step Up* with me on Sunday," Andrew said.

"Evening or matinee?" Dave asked.

"Matinee," Andrew said.

"Deal," Dave said.

Andrew nodded. Dave nodded. The only person who wasn't nodding was Eric. "I can't dance," he said.

Andrew rolled his eyes. "Everyone can dance. Just master one basic step to do with any song." He showed them three dance moves.

The first move relied on complicated foot-work — left, right, forward, back, left, right, spin — with arm swings and hip twists on every beat. "I'll never master that!" Eric complained. "Not even by the end of the year."

The second move was something Eric had seen two-year-olds do on YouTube: standing in place and bouncing with bent knees, while twisting the shoulders. "I'm not doing that for a three-minute song!" Eric whined. "Someone will pop a soother in my mouth."

The third move was just right: shifting the weight from side to side, swinging the arms forward and back in time with the opposite knee, and occasionally tapping a foot. It was easy, rhythmic, and hard to mess up. "The trick is keeping your face from looking insane," Andrew told Eric. "Try to keep your tongue in your mouth."

Eric was very slow in learning the steps. But Dave caught on right away. He added swivels, turns, pauses, and finger snaps. "You've got flair," Andrew told him.

"I've considered taking lessons," Dave admitted.

Nelson and Munster peeked around the corner while Dave and Eric were shaking their hips to Andrew's applause. The older boys roared with laughter. "Davy wants to learn to dance!" Nelson squealed.

"Maybe you should try out for cheerleading," Munster teased.

Mr. Papadakis crept up behind the eighth graders and shouted in his best punk rock scream, "This is not a grade eight area!"

Nelson and Munster shrieked and ran away.

Mr. P smiled. "Those two drive me nuts."

"One of them is my brother," Dave admitted.

"Sucks to be you," Mr. P said.

"We only have five minutes till the bell!" Eric whined. "I need more practice."

"Let's do free movement in gym class," Mr. P offered. "I've got some calls to catch up on." Scary noises blasted from his phone. "Want to dance to my band? I can get you a free download."

"Uh, great, yeah," Dave stammered. "Maybe when I delete some other songs and make some space?"

Mr. Papadakis cancelled geography and math to give his students the entire afternoon to practise dancing. He sat on a bench writing emails while the kids danced, played basketball, and got a Crazy Eights tournament going in one corner.

Dave, Eric, and Andrew practised in the equipment room. By the time the bell rang, they had their synchronized dance routine perfected. Eric even managed to keep his face under control through most of it. "There's no way I can mess this up," he said with a smile.

Dave patted his back and said, "You're a good dancer." He didn't like to lie but he knew that confidence was the only thing that could truly conquer fear — even if that confidence was based on a completely unrealistic assessment of one's skills.

#7:

Eventually you have to face the music.

A disco ball threw dots of light around the gym, spinning in time with the music. Mr. Papadakis stood onstage behind a DJ table, dancing wildly and shouting into his phone. Eight girls danced near the front of the room. Eighty other kids sat on benches along the walls or huddled in corners, talking loudly, shuffling their feet, and looking around nervously.

Dave, Eric, Taz, Nicolas, and Andrew stood by the wall, trying to appear at ease. Andrew sang along to the music. Nicolas bounced on his toes to the beat. Taz folded his arms across his *Reduce, Reuse, Recycle* T-shirt and frowned at the lack of adequate adult supervision in the room. Eric pressed the outside of his running shoe on the floor tiles and leaned his weight on it, hoping for a last-minute sprain.

"So you want to dance?" Dave said. "We should all just dance. This is a good song."

His friends stared at him like he was crazy.

Claire walked over with Vanessa and her little sister Jessica. "So you want to dance?" she asked. "We should all just dance. This is a good song."

"Yeah, yeah, sure," the boys said.

Nicolas raced onto the dance floor, dragging Claire by the hand. Once there, he threw himself into the air, shimmied in every direction, and played air guitar enthusiastically.

Taz offered his hand to Jessica and led her to the dance floor. Once there, he shuffled from foot to foot while shouting his concerns about stereotyping in hip-hop music.

Vanessa was left facing Dave, Eric, and

Andrew. She grimaced as if she couldn't decide which was the worst fate. Robbie strutted over sipping a slushie and swinging his bangs. "Want to dance, Vanessa?"

"With you, Robbie?" she said. "I'd love to."

Eric smiled as he watched them leave. "So far so good."

"Aw, nobody wants to dance with you!" Nelson teased as he walked by with Munster. "How sad. Davy's dance lessons were all for nothing."

"Not even," Dave said. "Let's go, guys."

Eric and Andrew followed Dave to the centre of the gym, right under the disco ball. They stood side by side — Dave smiling, Eric sweating, and Andrew snapping his fingers and counting, "One, two, three."

On the count of four, the boys began to swivel their shoulders left and right, with one arm bent upwards in front of them and the other arm bent behind them. They snapped their fingers and alternated sides every second beat.

After eight counts, they added some foot-work. They moved their left feet forward in time with their right arms, then their right feet forward in time with their left arms. After another eight counts, each boy crossed his left foot in front of his right and spun 360 degrees. They stretched out their arms and froze for four counts, then spun in the opposite direction. They were exactly synchronized, and their simple dance was the coolest thing going on in that gym.

Vanessa froze and watched with her mouth hanging open. Robbie dropped his slushie and left a puddle on the floor. Claire ran over to see better. Even Munster moved closer, clapping and counting the beats out loud. The clapping attracted the attention of the adults in the hallway. Eric's mother peeked inside the gym. She smiled with pride to see her son in the centre of the dance floor.

After repeating the same routine twice, Dave stepped in front of Andrew and Eric and showed off some robotic arm movements for sixteen counts. Then Andrew stepped out in front and showed off some taps and twists for sixteen counts.

It was Eric's turn to dance solo. And everyone in the gym was watching.

He completely forgot everything he'd planned to do. He took four steps backward, feeling for an exit, and bumped into Munster. He spun around, keeping time with the music, then froze in horror for exactly four counts. Still keeping the beat, he stumbled backward — one, two, three, four — then spun around and ran forward — one, two, three, four — until he hit the puddle of spilled slushie and began to slide.

Eric slid across the wet floor for a slick four counts — his arms stretched wide, his hands in stop position, the music blasting at his back. He saw his mother cheering him on from the gym doors and he fell to his knees before he reached her. He landed smoothly at the feet of two grade eight girls, who clapped and shouted, "Awesome move!"

Dave and Andrew danced over and helped Eric to his feet in four quick counts, then all three boys got back in step and ended the song together.

Everyone clapped. Mr. Papadakis held up his phone and shouted from the stage, "I just posted it to the class Facebook page! Great job, boys!"

"I need some air," Eric said, sweating and breathing hard. He ran out to the refreshment table, with his friends all following proudly.

"I always knew you'd be a good dancer," his mother said as she served his popcorn and juice. "I could tell by the way you kicked when you were in my belly."

Eric blushed and turned away.

"Eric is a great dancer!" Claire said. She smiled at Dave and added, "They're all great dancers."

The kids took their refreshments to a quiet spot down the hall. Eric leaned against a wall and sipped his juice. "I don't think I can do that again," he said.

"But you have to teach us your moves!" Nicolas said.

"We want to join your group dance," Taz added.

Andrew nodded. "I've got a lot more steps."

"I want to keep dancing, too," Dave said.

"Me too!" Claire added. "Come on."

Eric rose reluctantly.

They didn't see Nelson and Munster hiding on opposite sides of the gym doors, watching and waiting. The eighth graders stuck out their legs just as Dave and Eric walked through.

Dave was used to Nelson's tricks, so he side-stepped the trip easily. But Eric had no older brothers, so he walked right into it. He tripped over Munster's foot and fell to the gym floor, groaning. "Oh no! My ankle!"

His mother rushed over and helped him up. "It might be sprained, dear," she said. "You'd better sit out the rest of the dance."

Eric smiled. "If you really think I should."

Dave danced the night away, while Eric put his feet up and watched, eating popcorn and sipping cola.

"You're the king of the dance," Dave told Eric when the music finally stopped. "Everyone's talking about how I cured your fear of dancing. They say your slide was the best part of our routine."

Eric chuckled. "I know. It was a freak of nature."

"No. When you dance normally, *you're* a freak of nature," Dave said. "That was more like a freak accident."

"It was a freak of awesomeness," Eric said.

"Yes, it was. It was fearless."

"Thanks, Dave. I couldn't have done it without you."

October:

Dave Cures
Andrew's Fear
Of Public
Speaking

#8:

You're always speaking in public so watch what you say.

"You have to *what*?" Dave asked Eric. They were in the gymnasium storage room with Taz, Nicolas, and Andrew. It was lunch recess and Mr. Papadakis had let all five boys go inside to get one soccer ball. They'd been in the storage room for twenty minutes already. They'd had a bean bag war and a Hula Hoop contest, and now they were balancing pylons on their heads.

"I have to take dance lessons," Eric repeated. "It made my mom so happy to see me dancing, I didn't have the heart to tell her no."

"I wish I could take them with you," Dave said. "But my parents said no more lessons this

year. They're still mad about me dropping out of football and karate this summer."

"And gymnastics and painting in the spring," Eric added.

"And piano and drama last year," Taz said.

"And weren't you in yoga for a while?" Nicolas asked.

Dave sighed. "Okay. I have a two-week attention span." He grabbed a soccer ball from the mesh bag on the floor and put it on top of the pylon on his head. All of his friends placed balls on their pylon hats, too. Nicolas clicked his stopwatch and said, "Go."

"When do you start dance lessons?" Andrew asked Eric.

"November. My mom says my ankle should be healed by then."

Everyone looked down at the perfectly healthy ankle hiding above Eric's red sneaker. All the pylons and balls fell to the floor. "Oops."

"Twelve seconds," Nicolas announced. "Not bad."

"What's wrong with your ankle?" Andrew asked Eric.

"He's been faking a sprain all month," Taz said with obvious disapproval.

"He wraps it in a giant bandage before he gets home," Nicolas explained.

"He tells his mom how much he'd love to be dancing if only his ankle wasn't busted," Dave added.

"I'm too good of a liar," Eric sighed.

Nicolas spun a soccer ball on his index finger and everyone tried to copy him.

"I should get one of those bandages," Andrew said. "I wouldn't have to rake the leaves if my wrist was sprained."

"I wouldn't have to clean my room," Dave said.

"I wouldn't have to go to school!" Nicolas shouted.

"You guys have no idea I'm here, do you?" Mr. Papadakis asked from the doorway.

The boys jumped and screamed and dropped their balls.

Their teacher leaned against the door frame, texting. "You should do your speeches

on how to lie to grown-ups," he muttered, "since you're all so good at it."

"Speeches?" Andrew asked.

Mr. P tucked away his phone. "Yes, boys, it's public speaking time." He frowned. "Not right now, of course. It's lunch recess. But since you've taken twenty minutes to fetch a ball, let's call it a lunch detention, shall we? You can clean tables till twelve-thirty."

The boys grumbled as they followed Mr. P out of the gym, down the hall, and into their empty classroom. "You know where the rags are, right?" Mr. P asked.

They nodded sadly. Outside the windows, in the cool autumn sunshine, their classmates peered in at them, pointed, and laughed.

"Excuse me, sir, but I don't do speeches," Andrew said.

Mr. P snorted. "You do if you want to pass grade six." He assigned four dirty tables to each boy. "Just clean them," he said. "Don't balance them on your heads."

"Can I get out of the speech if my mom

writes a note?" Andrew asked.

"Is your mother a licensed psychiatrist or the prime minister of Canada?" Mr. P asked.

Andrew shook his head.

"Then no," Mr. P said. He opened a cupboard and passed Andrew a spray bottle.

"Do your speech on dancing," Dave suggested. "It'll be fun."

"It won't be fun!" Andrew said, turning pale and trembling.

"No. Speeches are never fun," Mr. P agreed.

"It's the most significant learning experience of the term," Taz said as he sprayed a table with soap.

Mr. P laughed. "I still think about poor Mitch Laurence from my own grade six public speaking competition." He pulled out his phone and added, "I wonder if he ever got out of the asylum."

"You're kidding, right?" Andrew asked.

Mr. P smiled and waved. "Scrub away, boys. Scrub away." His footsteps echoed down the empty hallway.

"I might do my speech on weird teachers," Taz said.

Andrew moaned. "I can't do a speech. No way. Uh-uh. I won't do it. I'm too scared."

Everyone turned to Dave.

"I can't get this table clean," he muttered. "Someone from last year wrote *Becky loves Carlos* in permanent ink along the side." He looked up at his friends and stopped scrubbing. "Why are you all staring at *me*?" he asked.

#9:

If it's exciting, it's probably not allowed in school.

Mr. P was late for class. The students gathered in small groups to chalk on the board, share snacks, and gab about their speeches.

"I'm doing Australian animals," Dave announced.

"I'm doing African animals!" Claire exclaimed.

She held her hand up for a high-five and Dave was just about to slap it when Nicolas crashed into him and said, "I'm doing skydiving."

"I'm doing bullying," Taz said. "That topic has a seventy per cent chance of winning no matter what I say."

"I can't decide between comic books, graphic

novels, or manga," Eric said. "They're all so different, it's hard to choose."

"What about you, Andrew?" Claire asked.

Andrew blinked rapidly. "I don't do speeches."

"I remember where I saw you before!" Vanessa shouted behind him.

Red blotches crept over Andrew's freckles, up his jaw toward his cheeks.

"You're that kid from Peterson Public School who threw up all over the podium last year!" Vanessa laughed. "I saw the video on Facebook!"

Andrew looked like he'd buried his face in a cherry pie.

Robbie pulled out his iPod and said, "Oh man, yeah! Let's look that up."

"No electronics in the classroom," Taz said, snatching Robbie's iPod. He was the only kid big enough to ever challenge Robbie.

"I heard about that poor kid," Dave whispered to Andrew. "That was you?"

Andrew shook his head. In fact, he shook everything: his hands, his legs, even his ears squirmed.

Mr. Papadakis entered the room. "Sorry I'm late. You wouldn't believe how much administrative work teachers have. You think it's going to be a nine to three job but man, there's a lot of overtime." He passed out a stack of blue papers. "Your parents have to sign this form saying they know your speech is due in two weeks. There'll be no excuses for not participating."

Eric held up his hand. "What if someone has a decapitating fear of public speaking?"

Mr. P squinted. "That sounds messy."

Dave raised his hand. "He means what if someone is so scared they puke?"

Mr. P's face turned white and he recoiled in horror. "There's absolutely no vomiting allowed in my classroom."

"But what if someone has a phobia of public speaking?" Taz said. "It would be a form of child abuse to force him to speak."

Mr. P snorted. "Come on, people. It's just a speech. Be creative with it. Problem solve."

The students stared at him blankly.

"Do your speech to music," he

suggested. "Or turn it into slam poetry or performance art or dramatic skits." He circled his hands in the air and smiled. "Don't give me those boring speeches kids always write. Give me something inspired."

Taz raised his hand. "This form says it's a three-minute speech based on fact with no props or cue cards allowed."

"Let me ask Ms. Samson." Mr. P dashed out of the classroom and across the hall.

"I could dance my speech!" Andrew said excitedly.

"We could do a group skit," Dave suggested to Claire. "We could be animal experts travelling the globe."

"We could skydive into different countries," Nicolas added.

The whole class buzzed with excitement.

Mr. P dashed back into the room. "No. Bummer. Sorry, kids. It's a three-minute speech, old-school style. You can bring one picture to display, but otherwise it's just you and the podium."

The whole class groaned.

Mr. P shrugged. "Sucks to be you. Take ten minutes to discuss your topics." He plugged in his earbuds and turned on his phone.

Andrew dragged his chair to Dave's desk. "I can't do it!" he whispered in panic.

"How can someone dance in front of a crowd, no matter how much they get laughed at, but be too scared to speak?" Eric asked.

"Who laughs at my dancing?" Andrew asked.

"Only jerks," Dave assured him.

As if on cue, Vanessa turned in her seat and sneered. "I can't wait for your speech, Andrew."

Robbie snickered and said, "Yeah. We'll bring barf bags."

Andrew looked at Dave. "Please help," he whispered.

"What can *I* do?" Dave asked.

"You helped Eric with his fear of dancing."

"I'm still afraid of dancing," Eric mentioned.

"But you got through the dance," Andrew said. "Dave can get me through the speech."

"I don't know," Dave said. "It's not like I'm an expert."

"I'll give you twenty-four tokens good for *Dance Dance Revolution* at the arcade," Andrew said.

"But I do have some skills," Dave said with a smile.

#10:

Handwashing is the best way to prevent the spread of germs.

"My neighbour told me a joke," Dave said on the bus to school. He looked from Eric, in the window seat beside him, to Andrew, in the seat across the aisle. "A man goes to the doctor. He says, 'Doctor, it hurts when I lift my arm.' And the doctor says, 'So don't lift your arm.'" He smiled and waited for a response.

"Is that the joke?" Andrew asked.

Dave nodded.

"It's not funny," Eric said.

"Of course not," Dave said. "My neighbour is ancient. The point is, if something hurts, don't do it. If public speaking makes you sick, don't speak in public."

#10: Handwashing is the best way to prevent the spread of germs

"I don't think this is proper therapy," Andrew said. "I was hoping for more. Eric got lessons and everything."

"Why go through the hassle of lessons?" Dave asked. "Just get excused from the competition."

"Mr. P said no excuses," Eric reminded him.

Dave waved a hand in the air. "There's always room for excuses. All you need is a medical emergency. Like a sprained ankle, but for speeches instead of dancing."

Eric frowned. "People don't sprain their tongues."

"No, but they lose their voices," Dave said. He turned to Andrew and said, "You can't speak if you can't speak, right?"

Andrew had to think about that one.

"My mom lost her voice once from a virus she caught like a cold," Dave said.

Andrew made a face. "I don't like germs. I'm a clean freak, actually. I shower every day. And I'm fussy about my hair."

Dave and Eric squinted at Andrew's red hair,

which swooped over his eyebrows and around his ears and clung there unmoving as if it were made of Lego.

"I use a bit of product," Andrew admitted. "But it's super-clean."

"So keep your hair clean but get your hands dirty," Dave said. "That's how you'll catch the best germs."

"What if I catch the wrong germs?" Andrew asked. "What if I don't lose my voice at all but I catch a horrible stomach sickness that makes me throw up in the middle of my speech?"

Dave shrugged. "Then you're back to square one."

"What if the germs make me mess my pants in the middle of my speech?" Andrew whispered. "That's worse than square one."

"I don't think there's a germ that makes you poop your pants during speeches," Eric said. "I'd have heard about it in my YouTube research."

"What if I don't catch any germs at all?" Andrew asked. "I'm incredibly healthy. I've never been sick a day in my life, if you don't count the times I've thrown up during speeches."

#10: Handwashing is the best way to prevent the spread of germs

"It's worth a try," Dave said as their bus pulled in to the school lot.

Eric took his camera out of his backpack. "I'm going to film this. I'll call it, *Birth of an Illness*."

They hopped off the bus and led Andrew around the school grounds, directing him to touch all the most germy places: monkey bars, hand rails, door knobs, taps, even tissues. "Use Taz's pencils," Dave said. "His little sister has a cold."

For two days, Andrew touched all things germy and never once washed his hands. He did not get any viruses. All he got was completely disgusting hands.

"Gross me out! Don't come near me with those!" Vanessa shrieked when Andrew passed her desk.

"What's with the black goo under your nails?" Robbie asked. "That is not cool, man."

"This will make an awesome YouTube video if I speed up the timing," Eric said, holding his camera inches from Andrew's hands. "The dirt will bloom from your fingers like a flower opening its petals to the sun."

"You are going to be one weird film director

when you grow up," Andrew told him.

On Friday, half the class came down with a cold. But Andrew was fine. "You mustn't touch your face enough," Dave said, sniffling. "Stick your fingers up your nose more often."

Andrew looked at his dirty hands. There was grime in every wrinkle and the black under his fingernails had taken on a blue haze. "There's no way I'd bring these things anywhere near my face," he said.

"Are you telling me you've been going around collecting germs but not putting them in your mouth?" Dave asked.

"All right, everyone," Mr. P whispered. He'd been coughing so much he'd lost his voice. "The topic of your speech has to be handed in by Monday. I expect to see some thought put into your choices." He placed a bottle of hand sanitizer on Andrew's desk. "You might want to choose hygiene as your topic," he suggested.

Andrew soaked in the tub for half an hour that night. He clipped and cleaned his fingernails before calling Dave. "Is there some other way to get laryngitis?"

#11:

If you want to keep a secret, don't post it on the Internet.

"Singers always lose their voices," Dave said. It was a rainy Saturday, and he was in his basement with Eric, Nicolas, Taz, and Andrew, supposedly writing speeches but actually watching music videos.

Andrew frowned. "I already get hassled because I dance and I have red hair. If I sing, too, Robbie and Vanessa will torment me."

"Sing the national anthem," Taz suggested. "No one can get mad at someone singing the national anthem."

Dave nodded. "But sing it in a punk-rock style to strain your vocal chords."

Between the five of them, they managed to

remember the words of the national anthem. Andrew belted it out in a clear, powerful voice.

"Lower," Dave said.

"Louder," Eric said.

"Raspier," Taz said.

"Angrier," Nicolas said.

"Don't even stick with the basic melody," Dave suggested. "Just shriek."

Andrew screeched at the top of his lungs, "Ohhhhh Caaanadaaaaa! Our home! And naaaaative laaaand!"

"That's kind of awesome," Nicolas said.

"You have an amazing voice," Taz agreed.

"Have you ever been on YouTube?" Eric asked.

"We're forming a band," Dave said. He dragged out all the musical instruments his parents had bought him over the years for lessons he'd dropped out of after two weeks. "We've got an electric guitar, a keyboard, a snare drum, a couple of rattles, a ukulele, and a kazoo. Help yourselves."

The boys spent the whole afternoon singing variations of "O Canada" and banging out accompanying notes. Nicolas pounded the snare

drum. Taz tapped on the keyboard. Andrew plucked the ukulele and screamed. Dave howled along with the guitar. Eric filmed it all, while shaking the rattles at random moments.

Dave's mom came downstairs covering her ears with her hands. "Your dad and I have to go out for a bit!" she shouted. "There's pizza on the table."

"Great! Thanks! Take your time," Dave shouted.

"We will," she said, fleeing from the noise.

It took just ten minutes to record a punk version of the national anthem. The boys soon moved on to a reggae version, a country ballad version, a rap version, and a coffee shop version that made Andrew break down and cry. "Oh my God, I just love this country so much," he said, wiping his eyes.

"We're an awesome band," Nicolas said. "We've only been playing for one day and we already have five songs!"

"What should we call ourselves?" Taz wondered.

"The Nationals," Dave said. "All our music will be remixes of the national anthem."

"Brilliant," Eric said. "An identifiable brand will get us more hits on YouTube."

"Dance videos get the most hits," Andrew said.

Dave peeked out the basement window. "Let's do a dance routine in the rain. It'll help you lose your voice." He found some umbrellas to use as props, and the boys headed outside.

Eric stood on the porch and recorded fifteen minutes of footage before the others were soaked through. "I can edit it tonight and post it tomorrow," he said, packing away his camera.

"Are you losing your voice yet?" Dave asked Andrew as they towelled off on the porch.

Andrew shook his head. "It's getting stronger from exercise. I can hold a note for twenty seconds and my range has expanded into three octaves."

"You might have to fake it," Dave said.

"Mr. P will never believe me if I just stop talking," Andrew said.

"So lose your voice slowly," Dave told him. "Start with a rasp."

Andrew lowered his voice and growled a whisper from the back of his throat. "Does this sound like I'm losing my voice?"

"It sounds like you're possessed by the devil!" Eric said.

Andrew recited the national anthem in a devil voice.

"That's the creepiest thing I ever heard," Taz said.

Nicolas giggled. "Let's make some prank calls."

They went inside and called Vanessa. She answered on the second ring.

"Hello, Vanessa," Andrew said in his devil voice. "Want to come over and play?"

Vanessa screamed, the boys broke into laughter, and Andrew hung up.

Twenty seconds later, the phone rang. "You know that's Vanessa," Dave said.

Nicolas grabbed the phone. He spoke in his best devil voice, which was nowhere near as creepy as Andrew's. It sounded more like a two-year-old with a cold. "Hello, this is the Hell Hotel," he said.

"Dave Davidson?" Robbie shouted. "I'm at Vanessa's and your stupid phone call scared her and she's going to tell her parents."

Nicolas passed the phone to Dave, who passed it to Andrew, who said in his creepy devil voice, "Hello Robbie. There's room for you at the Hell Hotel."

"Aargh! It really is the devil!" Robbie screamed.

"That voice will definitely get you out of the speech," Dave said. All his friends agreed.

On Monday morning, Andrew put his devil voice to the test. He walked up to Mr. Papadakis and growled, "Sorry, sir, but I'm losing my voice."

"I don't think you are," Mr. P said, pulling out his phone. "Let's put this up on the Smart Board, shall we?"

Eric's video of the Nationals singing an emo version of "O Canada" filled the screen. Rain fell in slow motion. Taz held a compass pointing north. Nicolas smashed a drumstick into a puddle. Dave waltzed with an umbrella. Andrew stood in the rain with his arms outstretched, wailing, "With glowing hearts we see thee rise!"

"You guys aren't bad," Mr. P said. "Who recorded your video?"

Eric raised his hand.

"Can you record the speeches next week?" Mr. P asked. "I'd love to post them on the class Facebook page."

"I'm losing my voice," Andrew repeated as his video image held a pure high note for twelve seconds.

Mr. P rolled his eyes. "I'll give you till tomorrow to choose your topic."

#12:

Being in grade six is bad for Your self-esteem.

"You have one last chance to get out of the speech," Dave said. He was in his basement with Eric, Nicolas, Taz, and Andrew, supposedly reciting speeches but actually watching TV. "All you need is a doctor's note saying it's bad for your self-esteem."

"Do you know any doctors who honestly think a speech could be demented to a kid's self-esteem?" Eric asked.

Dave smiled. "I've always believed school speeches were demented."

"What about your neighbour?" Andrew asked, looking out the basement window. "Would he sign a note?"

"Why not?" Dave said. "He's retired. I bet he'd love to do something useful."

They found Dr. Walton outside in his garden. "Do you trim that hedge every month?" Dave asked.

The old man smiled. "I'm afraid I'm fussy, son."

"Speaking of being afraid," Dave said, "if someone with really low self-esteem was afraid of public speaking, don't you think a public speaking competition would be bad for him?"

Dr. Walton let his hedge trimmers dangle at his side. "Who are we talking about?"

Dave glanced over his shoulder at his friends. They waved encouragingly. "Just say you knew a kid like that," he said. "Would you write a doctor's note saying that giving a speech would be bad for his self-esteem?"

"No," said Dr. Walton. "First of all, I'm a veterinarian, son. So unless you're talking about Maisy, I'm not the doctor you're looking for. And second of all, a boy's got to learn to face his fears. That's called growing up."

"But —"

"I know a therapist who could help you."

"It's not me," Dave said. "It's my friend."

Dr. Walton winked. "Sure it is."

Andrew raised his hand. "It's me."

Dr. Walton looked Andrew up and down. "Maybe there's something I can do."

Dave smiled. "Thank you, sir!"

Dave wasn't smiling the next day at school when Mr. Papadakis announced a guest speaker for Health class. "Dr. Walton is here to tell us how to face our fears and build our self-esteem." Mr. P sat down with his phone in hand. "They're all ears, doc."

"Public speaking builds self-esteem," Dr. Walton began. He proceeded to bore the class for thirty minutes with the details of every public speaking competition he'd ever entered and how they made him the man he is today.

"Some children have low self-esteem," Dr. Walton concluded. He raised his bony old hand and pointed straight at Dave. "Like Dave Davidson and his friend Andrew.

You kids can help these timid boys grow into brave young men by supporting their participation in the public speaking competition."

"Why not just paint a bull's-eye on your rear end?" Taz whispered.

Dave was too shocked to whisper back. Andrew shrank in his chair, blushing scarlet.

"Way to go, Dave and Andrew," Vanessa snickered.

"You're so brave," Robbie added, laughing.

Mr. P put down his cell phone and stood up. "Great talk, doc. I'll let the boys go first with their speeches next week. Why delay the opportunity to build a little self-esteem?"

Andrew laid his forehead on his desk. He stayed there while the rest of the class filed out for recess.

"So you have to speak in front of the class," Dave said. "I can train you for that."

"But what if I win?" Andrew asked. "What if I have to speak in front of the whole school and then the whole city?"

Dave did not think that was likely. "Choose a losing topic," he said. "Something no grown-up wants to hear about even for three lousy minutes."

"Like what?"

"Like farts."

"I can't do a speech on farts!" Andrew said.

Dave smiled. "Call it the digestive system. That way, if you puke, you're still on topic."

Andrew perked up. "Great idea!" He ran to tell the teacher.

"The digestive system?" Mr. P repeated suspiciously. "I can't wait."

#13:

Friends Should have
Your back, Your front,
and both Sides.

Dave and Andrew sat at Dave's kitchen table after school, actually working on their speeches. "So what is it you're afraid of?" Dave asked. "Throwing up? Forgetting the words? Sounding like an idiot?"

"All those things," Andrew said. "Now that you mention them. I can't stand the thought of everyone watching me while I mess up."

"So make them watch something else," Dave said. "You can have one picture, right? Make it so fascinatingly disgusting that people can't look away from it."

Dave and Andrew spent half an hour trying to draw a hamburger travelling through an intestine and turning into poop.

Dave's mom came home from work, looked at the drawing, and said, "Mmm, that makes me hungry."

Andrew stared up at her in horror.

His mom smiled. "It's a layer cake searching for chocolate ice cream. Isn't it?"

Dave laughed. "Yup. It really makes my mouth water."

"Keep up the good work," his mom said on her way to the garden.

Andrew held up the drawing and groaned. "This stinks."

Dave agreed. "We need more realism. Let's take Maisy for a walk." He grabbed a poop bag and a camera.

Maisy stopped at the park to do her business. Andrew watched her, cringing. "I'm not standing next to a picture of that while I give my speech. I'll throw up for sure."

"Hey, Dave!" Claire shouted from the swings, where she sat with Vanessa.

"Are you taking a picture of your dog's

poop?" Vanessa shouted.

"Of course not!" Dave tucked his camera in his back pocket and pulled out a poop bag. "I thought I might take some pictures to go with my speech, that's all."

"Oh yeah, we've seen a lot of Australian wildlife here today," Vanessa said.

Claire giggled. "You just missed three kangaroos and a crocodile."

Dave walked away with the poop bag and a mild case of depression. "Either we dump this back out and take its picture," he told Andrew, "or we find a picture of something more eye-catching."

"I don't think that's hard to find," Andrew said. "Maybe Eric can help. He's artistic."

They found Eric shooting hoops in his driveway with Nicolas and Taz. "Remember that gag gift I got you for your birthday?" Dave asked him. "Do you still have that?"

Eric shrugged. "What if I do?"

"Can Andrew use it for his speech?"

"Yeah, okay. Come on in."

The boys headed up to Eric's bedroom. It was a big room with a desk covered in drawings, stacks of books on the floor, and an enormous bookcase lined with assembled Lego sets.

"Holy cow, you have the Death Star!" Andrew exclaimed excitedly.

Eric reached into the back of his closet and pulled out a framed poster of Justin Jarvis, the teen rocker every sixth-grade girl adored. Justin stood on a beach at sunset, wearing only a swimsuit and a guitar.

"And you have a Justin Jarvis poster!" Andrew exclaimed just as excitedly.

Nicolas laughed. "I can't believe you kept that."

Eric blushed. "I'm too embarrassed to put it out with the garbage."

"It's all right if you want to keep it," Taz said. "You shouldn't feel ashamed of who you are."

"I don't want to keep it!" Eric said.

Dave held the poster up for Andrew. "No one will look at you while you're standing next to this," he said. "Just paste a picture of the digestive system over his shorts."

Eric smiled. "I knew Justin Jarvis had a purpose."

They found a picture of the digestive system online, printed it out, and pasted it over Justin's belly. Eric drew a poison cloud coming from Justin's backside.

"Perfect," Andrew said. "I can talk about the separation of air and solids at the end of the intestine. Now I just need to memorize my speech."

That wasn't easy, even with four friends helping. After forty-five minutes, everyone knew the speech by heart except Andrew. "I can't do it!" he cried.

"We could hold up encouraging words to build your self-esteem," Taz suggested.

"Can't you just hold up cue cards?" Andrew asked.

"Why not do both?" Dave said.

Andrew wrote down each sentence of his speech on a separate sheet of paper in large letters. Taz took a few extra sheets and wrote, *Way to go*, and *You're doing great*.

"Let's try it out," Dave said.

Nicolas held up the cue cards, Eric held a pretend camera, and Dave and Taz held up encouraging words.

Andrew rushed through his speech so fast that he was panting by the end. "How was I?" he asked.

"I didn't pay attention," Nicolas admitted. "I was distracted by Justin Jarvis."

"It was only two minutes," Dave said. "You need to slow down if you want to pass."

"I can't slow down," Andrew said. "I'm too stressed out."

"I'll get my mom," Eric said. "She teaches yoga and meditation."

Ten minutes later, the boys were all sitting cross-legged on the floor doing shoulder shrugs to release their tension. Eric's mother sat across from Andrew, smiling. She spoke in a low, slow, soothing voice. "Before you begin, imagine yourself standing in front of the class, completely relaxed and happy, and doing a wonderful job."

"I should write this down," Andrew said. He grabbed his notepad and pen.

"Don't worry about being watched," Eric's mom said. "The audience is there to support you. This is an opportunity to reach them."

"Don't worry about who's watching," Andrew repeated as he wrote.

Eric's mom smiled. "Remind yourself that you can do this. You control it. You can take it where it needs to go."

"You can do this," Andrew muttered as he wrote. "You control this."

"Any time worry creeps in," Eric's mom continued, "push it away. Take a deep breath and get back on track."

"Push it away," Andrew wrote.

"Relax your shoulders," Eric's mom said. "Relax your face. Relax your body. Smile. And just do it."

"Just do it," Andrew said as he wrote.

"We'll hold up these relaxation tips so you don't forget them," Dave said. He gathered Andrew's cue cards into one pile, and the tips and cheers into another pile. "What could possibly go wrong?" he asked.

#14:

Relax, release, and let go . . .

"Who wants to go first?" Mr. P asked the boys. "How about you, Eric? When you're done, you can film the others."

Eric gave a three-minute lecture on why school library collections should be made up of equal parts of manga, graphic novels, comic books, and a final category called "everything else."

"Very persuasive. As soon as our school can afford a librarian, we'll ask her to order those new collections," Mr. P said. "Next."

Taz gave a passionate anti-bullying speech. He quoted Jesus Christ, Mahatma Gandhi, Lady Gaga, and Lord Nelson Elementary School's

Principal Renault, who'd given her own anti-bullying speech the week before.

Mr. P clapped. "Great job. I'll make sure Principal Renault sees the video. It'll help with my performance review. Next!"

Dave described a long list of poisonous spiders, snakes, and fish, all in a bad Australian accent. "Even the duck-billed platypus is venomous," he said, concluding, "this is no country for wusses. G'day mates."

Claire gave him two thumbs up.

Nicolas appeared to make up his speech on the spot. "Some people think humans evolved on Earth after skydiving here from an alien ship," he began. It got weirder from there. Mr. P had to interrupt the final alien invasion before Nic destroyed the classroom.

"Go sit at the time-out table!" Mr. P told Nicolas. "You're up, Andrew."

Andrew faced the crowd and froze. He looked helplessly at Nicolas, who was no longer sitting at his desk where Andrew's cue cards and relaxation tips lay in heaps.

"Anytime you're ready," Mr. P said.

Andrew put one hand on his stomach and opened his mouth. It was impossible to say whether words or vomit were about to come out. Robbie snickered.

"Your poster," Dave whispered.

Andrew ran out to the hall and returned with Justin Jarvis, half-naked on a beach with his intestines showing. The boys giggled, the girls sighed, and no one stared at Andrew anymore. He took a deep breath and said, "Hello. Today I'm going to talk to you about the digestive system."

He paused for an awfully long time.

"Let's follow this burger," Dave whispered.

"Let's follow this burger," Andrew said.

Dave scribbled out the full sentence and held it up.

Andrew read, "Let's follow this burger on its journey through Jasbir."

"Justin," Dave whispered. He had messy printing.

Taz scribbled down the next sentence, and Andrew read, "We'll start at the point of entry, the mouth."

Everything went well that way for two minutes. Dave and Taz wrote out the lines and Andrew read them aloud. The burger travelled down Justin's throat, past his stomach, through his small intestine, and into his large intestine, where Dave and Taz ran out of memory. They knew how things ended, pretty much, but they didn't know how to say it.

Dave wrote, "We need a distraction."

Andrew said, "We need a distraction."

Dave shook his head frantically.

Andrew looked at the clock. He needed one more minute or he'd fail. He began to ad-lib through the tail end of the digestive system. "So yeah, like I said, the air gets separated from solids in the large intestine and passes out as gas." He pointed to Justin's backside. "Right about here."

Robbie snorted and Andrew froze. He couldn't think of another word to say. He stared at the papers on Nicolas's table like they might save his life.

Eric pointed his camera at the

wall behind Mr. P and shouted, "Look, it's a bird!"

As soon as Mr. P turned his head, Dave leaned across the aisle, scooped the papers from Nicolas's table, and sat back in his chair.

Mr. P stared from one boy to another.

"Sorry," Eric said. "It wasn't a bird."

Mr. P turned to Andrew. "Shall we complete the digestive process?"

Andrew nodded. He waited for Dave to hold up a cue card. He took a deep breath and read, "The most important thing is to relax. Don't worry if people are watching you."

"What?" Robbie shouted. "Who would be watching?"

Uh-oh. Dave turned around and saw the second pile of cue cards — the ones with the actual speech — tucked under Nicolas's binder.

Andrew, meanwhile, was staring blankly at the class. He felt sick to his stomach. All he could do was read the next paper that Dave was already holding up. "Tell yourself you can do this," he said. "You control this."

"I don't always control it," Nicolas said, giggling.

Dave shuffled through the papers in his hand. He stared back at Andrew, bug-eyed, and shrugged helplessly.

Andrew turned pale and wobbled.

Dave figured he could at least hold up some encouraging words.

Andrew steadied himself and read, "Just push it away."

"*Ew!*" the entire class groaned.

Dave put down the encouraging words.

Andrew gave a little shriek and held a hand over his mouth.

Dave looked at the clock. Fifteen more seconds. He didn't know what else to do, so he held up the next page.

Andrew read, "Take it where it needs to go. Just relax. Embrace this opportunity."

Half the class was giggling. The other half was grimacing. Even Mr. P had stopped multitasking and was staring at Andrew, waiting for whatever came next.

Dave flipped the page and Andrew read,

"Relax your shoulders. Relax your face. Smile. And just do it."

At the time-out table, Nicolas made a farting noise and shouted in a girly voice, "You did it, Justin!"

Everyone laughed.

"That's three minutes!" Andrew shouted joyfully. "I'm done! I didn't puke! Hallelujah! Phobia therapy saved my life!" He ran back to his chair.

"That was different," Mr. Papadakis muttered.

"That was the funniest speech ever," Dave said.

"You were awesome," Eric agreed from behind his camera.

Nicolas and Taz gave Andrew two thumbs up.

"You don't think I'll win, do you?" Andrew asked.

His friends broke out laughing. "No way!"

Andrew smiled. "Thanks, guys. I couldn't have done it without you."

November:

Dave cures
Vanessa's fear of
Dogs

#15:

Don't give people a reason to blackmail you.

"I'm not taking the bus today," Eric said when the school bell rang. He dragged his feet toward the front door.

"Me neither," Dave said. "I'm going to the library to play *Minemaker*. Want to come?"

Eric shook his head. "I have to go to my first dance lesson."

"Oh, yeah. Lucky you." They stepped outside into a grey autumn afternoon. "Is your mom picking you up?" Dave asked.

"No, I'm walking. I'll try to sprain my ankle on the way."

Dave furrowed his brow. "Is your mom driving you home after class?"

"No, I'll walk. I'll need the recovery time."

Dave stopped in his tracks. "So your mother won't actually see you at dance class? And no one there has met you yet?"

Eric stopped walking. "You're not going to suggest what I think you're going to suggest, are you?"

Dave smiled and held out his hand. "Nice to meet you. I'm Eric Leung. I love to dance."

Eric didn't shake hands. "You're Eric Leung? You're not even remotely Asian."

"I'm Irish-Chinese-Canadian. Didn't you know that? Come on. Let's switch places," Dave begged. "It's win-win. I get free dance lessons. You get to play *Minemaker*."

It was too good to resist. Eric slapped Dave a high-five and headed to the library. Dave headed to Samson's School of Dance.

"You must be Eric," a

muscular man said when Dave entered the studio. "I'm Chris. That's Isabel." He pointed to a tall woman standing behind a wall of little girls in leotards. "We're so happy to have a boy in the class," he added. "It's just you and fifteen girls."

Dave wondered if it was too late to call Eric back.

"Don't worry. There's no partnering," Chris said. "Today we'll learn the cupid shuffle."

Dance class didn't quite rise to Dave's hopes. But since he'd hoped to show off for twelve B-boys in cool uniforms who called him the best dancer ever born, that shouldn't have been surprising.

"Let's start over from the top," Isabel kept saying. The repetition reminded Dave of all the lessons he'd ever dropped out of: guitar, piano, golf, baseball, cartooning, origami. Wasn't there some life skill that didn't involve endless hours of practice drills? He was considering quitting when Chris patted his shoulder and said, "You're really good at this, Eric." All the girls in earshot smiled and giggled and said, "Yeah, you are." Dave decided to stay another week.

He only wished everyone would stop calling him Eric.

"Bye, Eric!" the girls shouted at the end of class.

Dave left the studio smiling. He walked straight into Robbie Templeton, who was dressed in a white uniform with a black belt, on his way to Sam Sung's Tai Kwon Do School next door. Dave had taken a week of lessons there when he was eight. He was surprised to discover that Robbie was a black belt. He didn't think Robbie had any hobbies except combing his hair and following Vanessa around.

"Eric, you forgot your school bag!" Chris shouted, passing Dave his bag.

"Eric?" Robbie repeated, staring at Dave.

"Nice belt," Dave said before he scurried away.

At school the next day, Mr. Papadakis announced, "It seems we were supposed to be studying ethics all term. My bad. I'll need your first written reports by Monday. Good luck."

Nicolas raised his hand. "What's ethics?"

"Moral standards," Mr. P said. Nicolas

gave him a blank look until he added, "Being good. Doing the right thing."

Robbie raised his hand. "We're adopting a rescued dog. That's morally good. Can I do my paper on that?"

Vanessa shrieked, "A dog? I hate dogs! I'll never visit you again if there's a dog in your house."

Robbie's jaw dropped. "You can't be serious."

Vanessa looked him up and down and snapped, "You better believe it. I won't go near dogs."

Eric pulled out his agenda and wrote at the top of his to-do list, *Get a dog.*

Dave raised a hand. "Can we work in groups?"

Mr. P smiled. "Yes. Groups of four. One report per group. Extra points to Mr. Davidson's group for that time-saving suggestion."

"That's not fair!" Taz shouted.

"Write out why it's not fair in eight hundred words," Mr. P said. "Hand it in Monday."

On Saturday, Taz wrote an essay on unfair

marking practices while Eric, Nicolas, and Dave played Frisbee in his yard. On Monday, they handed in the group paper. "I love ethics class!" Nicolas said.

On Wednesday, Dave went to his second dance class. He learned the wave, the jerk, and something called the Chris-cross, which he was pretty sure his teacher just made up. He aced it all. "I'll probably see you next week!" he shouted on his way out.

Robbie caught him by the sleeve. "Isn't it funny how no one in that dance studio knows who you are?" he whispered.

"Not especially funny, no," Dave said.

"Keep up the good work, Eric!" Chris shouted on his way to his car.

"Yeah, *Eric*," Robbie said.

Dave waited for Robbie to rat him out. But instead Robbie said, "I've heard about you curing all your friends of their fears. So now you're going to cure Vanessa of her dog phobia. Or else I'll tell your dance teacher who you really are."

Dave shrugged. "I was thinking of quitting, actually."

Robbie leaned into his face and said, "He'll tell Eric's mother, who will tell *your* mother all about your little switcheroo."

Dave sighed. "Okay, I'll do it." A wise man knows when he's been beaten.

#16:

If you make plans for other people, be sure to let them know.

"I'm not helping Vanessa Raymond!" Eric shouted into the phone after Dave told him about Robbie's blackmail scheme. "She ruined my childhood."

In kindergarten, Vanessa had pushed Eric off the top of the slide and told a yard supervisor that Eric had tried to kiss her. In later years, she'd put salt in his applesauce, performed a one-woman play called "Eric Leung Gets Eaten by Ants," and posted a picture of Eric picking his nose on the Lord Nelson Facebook page.

"What do you know about dog phobias, anyway?" Eric asked.

"Nothing. That's why I need your help.

You're Master of the Internet."

Eric sighed. "When is Vanessa's first session?"

"She doesn't actually know she's my patient yet," Dave admitted. "I'll let you know."

On Thursday morning, Dave took an indirect approach to Vanessa, which meant he totally avoided her and spoke to Claire instead. She was sipping at the water fountain. Dave hovered beside her.

"What's up?" she asked, wiping her lip.

"I was just thinking what a shame it is that Vanessa has a dog phobia," he said. "Once Robbie gets his dog, she won't go over to his house."

Claire furrowed her brow. "You were thinking about that?"

"Yeah, it's been bothering me," Dave lied.

Claire backed away slowly toward their classroom.

"You might have heard that I'm pretty good at curing people's fears," Dave said, following.

She nodded. "You're great at that."

Dave blushed. "So, um, you know, I was thinking I should cure Vanessa."

Claire leaned toward him and whispered, "I don't think Vanessa wants to be cured by you."

"She might if you were my helper."

"Really? You need a helper? What would I do?"

Dave had no idea. He raised his palms and said, "Calm the patient?"

Claire smiled sweetly. "Okay."

Dave smiled back. This blackmailing business might have an upside after all.

At lunch recess, Claire asked Dave to sit with her and Vanessa. He opened his sandwich box and said, "Did you know that some people are afraid of bologna? It's the most common sandwich phobia." He smiled and continued. "Fear of dogs is one of the most common animal phobias. You have that one, right, Vanessa?"

She gave him a withering look.

He pretended not to notice. "The first step to a cure is admitting that you have a problem," he said.

"I don't have a problem," Vanessa snapped. "Dogs are creepy and vicious and you'd have to be insane to go near one."

"My mom was talking about getting a dog," Claire said. "It would be terrible if you couldn't come over because of that, Vanessa." She paused and suggested gently, "Maybe Dave could help you feel more comfortable around dogs."

Vanessa sighed. "What would *he* know about making people feel comfortable?"

"I think you should write out your therapy plan, Dave," Claire said. "Then Vanessa will know what to expect."

"My therapy plan?" Dave repeated.

Claire nodded.

"Uh, sure. I can get you that tomorrow."

Eric came over after school to help Dave develop a therapy plan for curing dog phobias. After ten minutes of Internet surfing, Eric said, "Looks easy enough."

Dave agreed. "Want to play *Minemaker* now?"

#16: if you make plans for other people, be sure to let them know

On Friday morning, Dave cornered Vanessa at the water fountain. "Animal phobias are easily cured with exposure therapy," he said. "You should try it."

"What's exposure therapy?"

"It's when you expose yourself to the dog." There was an uncomfortable silence until Dave explained, "You just have to be near it. We'll use Maisy. She's gentle."

Vanessa gasped. "I'm not going near your giant dog!"

"We'll start slowly," Dave said. "I won't lock you in a room with her right away."

Vanessa poked his chest with her index finger. "You won't lock me in a room with your dog *ever*. If you even *think* of locking me in a room with your dog, I'll devote the rest of my life to your humiliation."

"That would take the heat off Eric, at least" Dave said, with a smile that Vanessa did not return. He cleared his throat. "Okay, we'll start your therapy by looking at pictures of dogs. Then we'll work up to hugging Maisy."

"I'm not hugging your dog!" Vanessa shouted. "She could swallow my whole head."

"She's thirteen years old. You could outrun her."

"Not if my head was swallowed."

Dave sighed. "I can cure you of these negative thoughts in just a few hours. Or possibly four weeks." He wasn't going to treat Vanessa's phobia one second longer than his dance lessons lasted.

"Why four weeks?" she asked.

"That's the moral standard," he said. "You know, like we're learning in ethics class."

"Helping people has a four-week time limit?"

"Yup."

Vanessa nodded. It seemed reasonable. "What would I have to do?"

"We'll work through a hierarchy of fears, from easy things to scary things."

"I'm never hugging your smelly old dog."

"Let's concentrate on the easy things for now," Dave said. "Come over to my house with Claire and look at pictures of dogs. You can do that, right?"

She rolled her eyes. "As long as you're not in the picture."

#17:

Too many therapists spoil the patient.

At school on Monday, Mr. P announced, "Everyone has to ask one ethical question. We'll discuss the answers as a group."

Robbie stared at Dave and asked, "Why is it wrong to pretend you're someone you're not?"

Dave stared at Robbie and asked, "Why is it wrong to rat out your classmates?"

Nicolas stared at Claire and asked, "What's your favourite ice cream flavour?"

Mr. P frowned. "We might have to review the definition of ethics. You have a second report to do this month."

After school, Vanessa, Claire, and Eric gathered in Dave's basement. Vanessa stretched out on the couch. Claire sat in the armchair. Dave and Eric squished onto a footstool. "First we need to find out where your fear came from," Dave said.

"Dave! Your stupid band is here!"  Nelson called down.

"Shoot," Dave said. "I forgot about band practice."

Nicolas, Taz, and Andrew hopped downstairs.

"I didn't sign up for group therapy," Vanessa complained.

"They're here to work on a heavy metal version of the national anthem," Dave explained. "Just ignore them."

It's hard to ignore a heavy metal version of the national anthem.

"Your band stinks!" Vanessa shouted over the pounding snare drum.

Dave concentrated on his list of questions. "Have you ever had a bad experience with dogs?" he shouted.

Andrew put down his microphone. "I was chased by a whole pack of dogs when I was little," he said. "I was playing in the yard when four dogs raced down the street right at me. I barely made it inside alive."

Vanessa stared at Andrew in horror.

"Thanks for that input into Vanessa's therapy," Dave said. "Question two: Did you ever see someone else have a bad experience with dogs?"

Nicolas put down his drumsticks. "I just saw a movie about scary dogs," he said. "A plane full of sled dogs crashes in the woods and the dogs get so hungry they try to eat the survivors. They drag an old lady away by the arm!"

Vanessa put a hand over her mouth.

"That's another helpful contribution," Dave said through gritted teeth. "Question three: Did your parents ever tell you that dogs were dangerous?"

"My mom always told me to stay away from dogs," Taz said, shutting off the keyboard. "When she was a little girl, her friend was attacked by their neighbour's guard dog. It bit her right in the face."

"Just go play a song!" Dave shouted.

"Let me tell *my* story!" Vanessa said. She took a deep breath and rubbed her hands together. "Okay. So two summers ago I went for a bike ride. I had a mountain bike that used to be my brother's, with stupid orange streamers in the handles. I was wearing flip-flops and a sundress and I was biking home from my friend's house." She turned to Claire and asked, "Remember Gloria Fielding? She had curly, brown hair and she talked in a really high voice?"

Claire nodded.

"Is there a dog in this story?" Dave asked.

Vanessa glared at him. "Yes! A dog raced down someone's driveway, barking at my bike, and my flip-flop caught in the chain so I fell off and broke my wrist." She held out her left wrist for everyone to see. "I was in a cast for, like, six weeks."

Dave frowned. "It sounds like you should be afraid of bicycles and flip-flops instead of dogs."

"Your therapy stinks," Vanessa said.

"Let's get to the harkening of fears," Eric suggested.

"Hark, I hear the fear approaching," Dave said, smiling. He passed Vanessa a dog magazine. "Step one. Look at pictures of dogs."

Nicolas and Claire squished in close on either side of Vanessa on the couch, smiling at the dogs in the pictures and pointing out favourite breeds.

Vanessa turned a page. "It doesn't really scare me to look at pictures."

"Good," Dave said. "Step two is to touch the pictures."

Vanessa cringed when she touched the photos of larger breeds. "I don't really like this."

"That means the therapy is working," Dave said. "You're doing great."

Andrew rolled his eyes. "I have to leave in ten minutes. Do you want to record the anthem or not?"

"Sure. That's enough therapy for today," Dave said. "Good work, Vanessa. Be sure to tell Robbie about your progress."

"That's it?" Vanessa whined. She rose from the couch and complained, "Ew! My pants are covered in dog hair!"

She walked through the kitchen and groaned, "Ew! I stepped in something wet!"

"That would be drool," Dave told her.

She stopped at the front door and said, "If I step in dog poop, your therapy days are over."

"Stick to the walkway," Dave advised her.

"Maybe we should meet in the park next session," Claire suggested.

Vanessa glared at Dave. "You'd better know what you're doing by then."

#18:

Slow and steady doesn't get you far but you get there steadily.

Dave and Eric walked to the dollar store on Saturday morning. Eric bought bubble gum, two chocolate bars, and a set of army men that wouldn't stand up. Dave bought Bristol board, elastic ribbon, and shaggy, brown bath mats. "For dog masks," he explained.

They brought their goodies back to Dave's house and laid them out in the basement. They cut up the bath mats and pasted the pieces onto Bristol board cut in the shape of snouts and ears. They fastened them onto their heads with elastic.

"We look so weird and creepy," Eric said in front of the mirror. "I'm getting my video camera."

Dave nodded. "Let's get the guys together. I feel an anthem coming on."

Nicolas, Taz, and Andrew met them in the park. Dave passed them each a dog mask.

"Vanessa's not going to pet us, is she?" Taz asked while he fastened on his ears.

Eric set up his tripod and suggested, "Let's try a howling version of 'O Canada'."

They filmed all possible combinations of four boys on swings: sitting, standing, lying on their bellies, swinging in the same direction, swinging in opposite directions, and staying still. Finally, everyone twisted his swing as tightly as he could. On Eric's count, they let the swings unravel in a synchronized spin while they raised their heads in a group howl.

"We are so artistic," Andrew said. He stood up and wagged his butt at the camera.

"Let's rewrite the anthem from a dog's perspiration," Eric suggested.

"Do dogs sweat?" Dave asked.

"You know what I mean," Eric said.

"We'll change the words to what a dog would say. I'll add some footage of real dogs to the video."

"Great idea," Nicolas said. "We can do tricks, like cartwheels and handstands, and then show real dogs doing tricks, too. My dog can jump through a Hula Hoop."

"Maisy can give a high-five," Dave said.

"My neighbour's dog can roll over," Andrew said.

"It's going to get all kinds of hits on YouTube," Nicolas said. He climbed the swings and hung upside down in his dog mask. "Are you getting this?" he shouted.

"Totally," Eric said, filming.

Dave turned to Taz. "You're a good writer. Can you do a dog anthem?"

Taz nodded. "I'm already working it out in my head. It's called 'O Can-of-food'."

"Why stop at dogs?" Eric said. "Let's do a cat anthem and soar to the top of the YouTube charts."

"O *Cat*ada!" Taz shouted.

"We catch our mice for thee!" Dave cried.

The afternoon wore on with dog, cat, mouse, squirrel, deer, and skunk versions of the national anthem. The skunk anthem was composed mostly of farts. "It'll be our greatest hit," Nicolas said.

"So when's Vanessa coming?" Andrew asked.

"Oh, yeah," Dave said from the top of the jungle gym. "It's possible I got distracted."

"Let's visit her in our dog costumes," Nicolas suggested. He looked Taz up and down and said, "You're an awfully big dog. You should be on a leash."

"That's disrespectful," Taz said.

Dave wasn't so sure. "A leash is a good idea. The appearance of control is very important in curing phobias."

Taz pointed a finger at him. "You're not putting anyone on a leash. Not while I'm here." He scratched under his dog snout and added, "I'll make sure we keep our dignity."

"Okay, no leashes," Dave said. "But I get to be the human master leading the pack of dogs." He helped Eric pack his camera, then led the way to Vanessa's house. He had to scold Nicolas three times for barking and once for chasing a cat.

When Vanessa answered her door, Dave

said in bad German accent, "Unt now I vill cure you of your crazy doggie fears."

Nicolas wagged his bottom and barked. Andrew snapped at him. Taz growled. Eric howled.

"Bad dogs!" Dave shouted. "Go lie down!"

Vanessa closed the door in their faces.

Robbie opened the door seconds later and whispered, "You better work harder than this, Davidson, or you'll be exposed."

#19:

Puppies are just not scary.

"My mom keeps asking to see my dance moves," Eric told Dave in the schoolyard on Monday morning. "I'm still taking lessons, right?"

Dave made a face. "You're getting tired of kick-stepping to Justin Jarvis tunes, actually."

"What does that mean?" Eric asked.

The bell rang and Dave just shrugged and headed toward the lineup.

"Wait a minute!" Eric said, following him. He grabbed Dave by the coat sleeve and said, "Eric Leung doesn't quit things."

Dave pulled his arm free. "He might be picking up some new habits. Sorry. He might not have time for dance lessons now that he's in a band." He shuffled through the doors and down the hallway.

Eric followed, dragging his feet. "I wasn't thinking when I let you pose as me," he said sadly.

Dave snorted. "You weren't thinking when you told your mom you love to dance."

They stopped outside their lockers and glared at each other. Then Dave said, "We should do our new ethics essay on this moral dilemma."

"No way," Eric said. "Mr. P might tell our moms." He paused for a moment, then suggested, "Let's do our essay on Vanessa's phobia therapy. Helping people overcome phobias is ethical, right?"

"Not if you're being blackmailed into it."

Eric shrugged. "We could leave that part out. Maybe we can make it a video-essay."

Dave agreed. "Mr. P will love that idea."

Not only did Mr. P love the idea of a video-essay, he even offered to let them use class time for Vanessa's third therapy step: Watch a movie about dogs. He caught up on emails while his class watched *Puppies on Mars*, followed by an exclusive showing of the Nationals' "O Can-of-food" video.

As the anthem ended in a long group howl, the classroom exploded with applause — or at least that section of the room where Nicolas sat.

"*This* is Vanessa's therapy?" Robbie whispered, scowling.

Dave nodded. "It's really helping her."

They turned to Vanessa, who was doodling *I Hate Dogs* all over her agenda.

"She's ready for step four," Dave said. "The pet store."

After school, Vanessa and Claire walked to the mall with Dave and Eric. Four fluffy black-and-white puppies played in the pet shop display window. Three of them tumbled and chased each other while the fourth trembled in a corner. The sign on the glass read *Shih Tzus*, which Dave and Eric repeated endlessly.

"I never knew a Shih Tzu could be so cute," Eric said.

Dave nodded. "I could take a Shih Tzu home."

"I would like to have a Shih Tzu right now."

"Sometimes it helps to have a Shih Tzu."

"Watch out!" Eric shouted. "Don't step on the Shih Tzu."

Vanessa rolled her eyes. "You little Shih Tzus better get on with my therapy."

Dave pulled out his hierarchy of fear. "Step four is to stand near a puppy behind glass. Step five is to stand near a puppy on the ground. Step six is to touch a puppy. And Step seven is to hold a puppy."

Vanessa squinted at the pet shop window. "Seriously?"

"Are you scared to move closer?" Dave asked.

"To those things? Who could be scared of them?"

"You're not afraid at all?" None of Dave's Internet research had prepared him for this.

"They're squirrel-size," Vanessa snorted.

"So it wouldn't bother you to go up to the glass?" Dave asked.

Vanessa walked up to the glass.

"You don't feel any stress?" Dave asked.

Vanessa shrugged. "No."

"Try touching the glass while you look

at the dogs," Dave said.

Vanessa put both hands on the window. One of the bolder pups jumped up and pawed the glass. Vanessa made a face like she'd eaten a lemon. "They're not scary," she said. "They're just gross."

"They're adorable!" Claire exclaimed.

Dave approached the sales clerk. "Could we see the puppy in the corner, please? The shy one?" The clerk set the trembling pup on the counter. It buried its little black nose in Dave's sweatshirt, looking for a place to hide. "It's important to expose yourself to a calm animal," he told Vanessa as he coaxed the little dog to look up.

"I'm not exposing myself," she said. "Let's get that straight."

"He's so cute!" Claire exclaimed. She leaned close and scratched under the pup's chin, whispering, "Hey there, sweetie. Aren't you a good little dog?"

"Come stand beside him," Dave urged Vanessa.

She inched closer.

"Isn't he cute?" Claire asked.

Vanessa wrinkled her nose. "It looks like it belongs in a toy store. At the back. In a bargain bin."

"Can you touch him?" Dave asked.

Reluctantly, she reached out her hand and stroked the puppy's back. "It's not very soft," she complained.

"Can you hold him?" Dave asked.

"Do I have to?"

"I'll help," Claire said. She took the puppy gently in her arms. "Don't be scared."

"I'm not scared!" Vanessa snapped.

"I'm talking to the dog," Claire said. "Hold out your arms."

Vanessa made a basket with her arms, and Claire laid the puppy inside. It squirmed and whimpered. "Stop clawing me!" Vanessa shouted.

"Please don't yell at the dogs," the sales clerk told her.

"There, there," Claire soothed, petting the puppy's head. "Don't listen to the mean girl."

Vanessa stretched her neck as far from the pup as it would go. "What do I do now?" she asked.

Dave stalled for time. He hadn't expected her to zoom through steps four to seven so quickly. "Um, now you rest. You've been under a lot of stress, even if you're not aware of it. You need a break before the next step."

"What's the next step?" Vanessa asked.

"I have to check. It might be meeting Maisy."

Vanessa looked down at the tiny dog in her arms. "How is this preparing me for that?"

Dave didn't have a clue. He faked a smile. "You'd be surprised."

"Whatever." Vanessa plopped the puppy on the counter. "I'm going to the candy store. Come on, Claire."

Claire scratched the puppy's head one last time. "Bye, sweetie!"

"Is nobody buying this dog?" the sales clerk asked.

"I would never buy a puppy from a pet shop," Claire said. "I'd adopt one instead."

"Man, that ethics class is really leaving a mark," Dave said.

#20:
Don't rush things.

Dave was tired of dance lessons. And he was tired of living a lie. He walked into Samson's studio on Wednesday, prepared to tell Chris and Isabel that he had to leave immediately to go live with his sick grandmother in Winnipeg.

"Hey, Eric," Chris greeted him. "Today we'll learn to moonwalk."

Dave paused with his mouth open. He didn't know anyone who could moonwalk. Nelson was always trying it and failing. Even Andrew couldn't do it. Dave imagined himself moon-walking from his locker to his desk, from his kitchen to his living room, from his house to Claire's, while the world stared in awe. "That's what I'm here for," he said.

After class, Dave moonwalked to the library and took out a book on phobias.

"You're spending a lot of time at the library these days," his mom said when he arrived home.

"No. This is the first time in ages."

His mother frowned. "Weren't you there last Wednesday? And the Wednesday before?"

"Oh, yeah. Sure." He smiled and said, "Wow, time flies. It feels like ages ago."

His mom set down her work and frowned. "Where have you been on Wednesdays, Dave?"

"Um, well, uh, you see . . ." After two minutes of stuttering, Dave spilled the beans.

His mother was furious. "What if there was an emergency and I had to reach you? What if something happened to you? I wouldn't even know where to look! You lied to me, Dave! And to your teachers. And to Mrs. Leung."

"I'm sorry," he said. "Please don't tell Eric's mom. It was my idea."

"You can tell her that yourself." She grabbed her coat and purse. "Let's go."

When they arrived at the Leung's house, Eric opened the door, took one look at Dave's face, and said, "I knew this day would come."

With a great deal of foot shuffling, head hanging, and tear wiping, the boys explained what they had been up to every Wednesday after school.

Eric's mother could hardly believe it. "Why would you pretend to like dancing?"

"It made you so happy," he said.

She just shook her head in disappointment.

"Dave will devote his allowance for the next three months to paying you back for the lessons," Dave's mother told Eric's mother. She turned to Dave and said, "And he will certainly be attending the last class."

Dave shuddered. His mother really knew how to dish out punishment.

Eric was grounded from *Minemaker* and all other video games for a month.

Dave tried to cheer him up by saying, "At least we don't have to cure Vanessa's phobia now that Robbie can't blackmail us."

Eric glared at him. "We still have to cure her. It's our ethics project."

#20: Don't rush things

The next night, Dave called Eric. "There are a lot of steps left to cure Vanessa. She's supposed to go from puppies to little dogs, then medium dogs, then big dogs. Where am I supposed to get all those dogs?"

"Ask Mr. P if we can have a bring-your-pet-to-school day," Eric suggested.

"Great idea," Dave said.

Mr. Papadakis dashed their hopes the next morning. "Sorry, boys. No animals on school property. I'm already bending the rules with the video-essay due next Friday."

"Friday?" Dave repeated. He turned to Eric. "We don't have time for little dogs or medium dogs." He raced outside to the soccer field where Vanessa and Claire were playing.

"Emergency therapy after school at my house!" he shouted. "We will face your fear and slay it! You're ready for the final step!" He held his arm out in a fist pump that no one returned.

Claire kicked the ball down the field. Vanessa shouted, "Stop bothering us in public!"

Eric joined Dave on the sidelines. "What's

Vanessa's final step?" he asked.

"Pet a large dog on the head."

Eric frowned. "You know the patient has to want it or it won't work, right?"

Dave nodded. "I have a plan. Don't worry. I may not know phobias, but I know Vanessa Raymond."

After school that afternoon, Eric, Claire, and Vanessa gathered in Dave's basement. Eric steered Claire to the craft table and showed her how to draw manga. Dave stood beside the couch and motioned for Vanessa to sit.

She plunked down with a huff. She crossed her arms and scowled. She said, "I'm not touching your giant dog. She better be locked up somewhere."

"She's upstairs," Dave said. "Tell me when you're ready and I'll bring her down."

"I'll never be ready."

"Whatever," Dave said, walking away. He put on some music and practised his moonwalk.

"Aren't we going to do some therapy?" Vanessa shouted.

"Whenever you're ready," Dave shouted back without even glancing at her.

After five minutes of being ignored, Vanessa was furious. "I didn't come here to watch you dance!" she yelled. "I came here for some therapy."

Dave waved a hand. "Whenever you're ready to meet Maisy."

After ten minutes of being ignored, Vanessa was miserable. "I might be ready to meet your stupid dog soon!" she yelled.

Dave tried not to smile.

"Genius," Eric muttered.

"Dave! Your stupid band is here!" Nelson shouted from upstairs.

"Oh no," Dave said. "I double-booked again."

Andrew, Nic, and Taz came downstairs. "Did you cure Vanessa's dog phobia?" Taz asked. The question caught Nelson's attention at the top of the stairs.

"She'll be cured when she's ready," Dave

said. "Let's start practising. You should film us, Eric."

Nelson peeked downstairs. He saw Vanessa sitting alone on the couch making faces at a dog magazine. He snickered.

Nelson fetched a handful of dog biscuits from the kitchen. He looked around the house for Maisy and found her lying on the bath mat, silently farting. He waved the biscuits in front of her face and led her to the basement door. He tossed the biscuits down the stairs and said, "Let the therapy begin."

Vanessa moped on the couch. "It's no fair that you guys are ignoring me. Why don't you film my therapy instead of your stupid band?" She lay back and closed her eyes.

"Maisy's keen ears heard Vanessa moaning under the music. The dog recognized the sound of a human in need of comfort. She thought a little nuzzling would cheer that girl right up.

"What on earth is that horrible smell?" Vanessa muttered. She opened her eyes and saw a big, shaggy, hundred-pound dog loping toward her.

Frozen in fear, she couldn't run. She couldn't stand. She couldn't even scream.

Maisy shuffled over to the couch, wagging her tail. She began to lick Vanessa's face. Her smelly breath shot into Vanessa's nostrils. Her sticky drool clung to Vanessa's cheek. Her furry chin tickled Vanessa ear. The more distressed Vanessa seemed, the more enthusiastically Maisy kissed her.

"Vanessa's cured!" Claire shouted from across the room.

Eric turned his camera on Maisy nuzzling Vanessa's neck. Everyone fell silent and stared.

"Do you feel any stress?" Dave asked.

Vanessa squeaked a little. Maisy put one paw on her shoulder to get a better licking position.

"This is a great ending to our video," Eric said.

Nelson snickered from the stairs. "Unless Maisy rips your friend's throat out."

Vanessa found her voice in that instant. She bolted upright and ran screaming from the room. She ran screaming out the door. She ran screaming all the way home.

"Mr. P is going to fail us for sure," Eric muttered.

"Poor Vanessa," Claire said.

"I'll call and apologize," Dave said. He picked up the phone and dialed Vanessa's number. "Hey, it's me, Dave, calling to say how brave you are."

"Your dog tried to rip my throat out and you just let her!" Vanessa yelled on the other end of the line. "I'm telling everyone you're a lousy therapist."

"She was kissing you!" Dave said. "There was no reason to be scared. You faced your worst fear. A big dog licked your face and nothing bad happened."

"Nothing bad happened?" Vanessa shrieked. "Eric has a video of me screaming like a fool!"

Dave paused for a moment. "So, you admit that you were foolish?"

#21:

Success may be just around the corner . . .

The following Wednesday, Dave went to his last dance class. It was awful now that everyone knew he was a liar named Dave. The girls wouldn't even look at him.

"Be sure to sign up for next term, everyone," Chris said when the hour was over. He turned to Dave and added, "Except for '*Eric*'."

Dave hung his head. "I'm sorry," he said. "It's not like I wanted to lie. I just wanted to dance."

Chris handed him his school bag. "Maybe we'll see you again sometime under your own name," he said.

Dave smiled. "Maybe. Bye!" He moonwalked out into the lesson-free world.

Robbie waited on the sidewalk, wearing his Tai Kwon Do uniform. His belt looked even blacker than before. "Your stupid therapy ruined everything!" he yelled. "Vanessa won't come over to meet Caesar. She says I'm her enemy because I have a dog. You just made things worse!"

Dave sighed. The sun was going down and there was a chill in the air, and he just wanted to get home and snuggle up with his PlayStation. But he'd taken enough ethics classes to know that, when you make a mess, you should clean it up. "I might not be as good at curing phobias as people have suggested," he admitted.

"But you have to cure her!" Robbie whined. "She'd love Caesar if she just gave him a chance."

Dave sighed. "What kind of dog is Caesar, anyway? A pitbull? A Doberman pinscher? A German shepherd?"

"He's a baby ShiChi," Robbie said. "Half Chihuahua, half Shih Tzu."

"Is that a joke?" Dave asked.

Robbie scowled. "Of course it's not a joke. He was rescued from a puppy mill. There's nothing funny about it."

"So he's a puppy?" Dave asked.

Robbie nodded. "He's ten weeks old. He's so small he fits in my hand."

Dave laughed. They might be able to salvage their ethics essay after all. "Vanessa aced puppy therapy," he told Robbie. "Bring your Shih Tzu to the park after school tomorrow and I'll introduce them."

Robbie grabbed his shoulder. "He's a ShiChi, Davidson. If you ever call him a Shih Tzu again, I'll bust your nose."

Fair enough, Dave thought. But in his head, he'd be calling Robbie's dog a little Shih Tzu.

After school on Thursday, Robbie met Dave, Eric, and Claire in the park. He held a baseball cap upside down in both hands. "Where's Vanessa?" he asked.

"She refused to come here," Dave said. "She seems to have developed a phobia of me. We'll have to go to her house. Where's Caesar?"

"In my hat." Robbie held out his ball cap. Inside it, a beige-and-brown puppy slept on its back, its paws neatly folded above its plump pink belly.

"Oh my goodness, he's so tiny!" Claire exclaimed, giggling.

"Don't laugh at him!" Robbie said. "He's had a tough life. Be nice."

Dave was finding Robbie's moral standards inconvenient. It was hard to keep on hating a guy who protected a puppy.

They walked together to Vanessa's house. Robbie spoke to Caesar in baby talk the whole way there.

Eric was very pleased to get that on camera.

Claire rang Vanessa's doorbell. "Stay behind me," she told Dave, "or she'll never open the door."

"You're sure she's not going to scream?" Robbie asked. "That would scar Caesar for life."

"She'll be fine," Dave said. "She did her therapy steps one to seven with no problem."

"Maybe you actually know what you're doing," Robbie said.

Dave nodded, forgetting momentarily that he didn't have a clue.

"Why did you bring *him*?" Vanessa snapped when she answered her door.

Dave peeked up from behind Claire's

shoulder. "We want you to meet someone," he said.

Robbie held out his hat. "This is Caesar."

"That's Caesar?" Vanessa repeated. She pursed her lips and squinted at the tiny creature that trembled before her. "He fits in your hat."

"You don't think he's scary?" Robbie asked.

She laughed.

"See how she's totally cured of her fear of your dog?" Dave said. He turned to Eric and asked, "You're filming this, right?"

Eric gave him a thumbs-up.

"You're not scared to touch him?" Robbie asked Vanessa. He lifted the hat a little closer to her.

Vanessa reached in and pet the top of Caesar's head. She smelled her hand and made a face.

Dave posed in front of the camera and asked, "So how did we do in treating your dog phobia, Vanessa? Remember, this is for ethics class."

Vanessa glared at him.

"Try picking him up," Robbie told her. "It'll help you bond."

"Go on," Claire encouraged. "Show everyone that you're not afraid."

Vanessa picked up Caesar and held him close to her face. She faked a smile and said, "I'm completely cured!"

"And that's a wrap," Eric said. "Good job. I think we'll get an A."

Vanessa plopped the dog back in the hat and said, "You don't deserve it."

"You're really not afraid of my dog?" Robbie asked.

She snorted. "Who could be afraid of that thing?"

Robbie gasped and covered Caesar's ears with the tips of his fingers. "Don't call him a thing! You'll hurt his feelings."

She rolled her eyes.

"You'll learn to love him," he said.

She looked down at Caesar like that was a highly improbable outcome for their relationship.

"So you'll come over on Saturday?" Robbie asked.

"Sure," Vanessa said.

Robbie turned to Dave and said, "Thanks, man. You're pretty good at phobia therapy."

Dave smiled proudly. "I prefer to call it fear-slaying."

December:

Dave cures claire's
fear of the future

#22:
A fair isn't always fair.

It was a snowy Monday morning, and Dave was late for school. "Sorry," he told Mr. Papadakis. "I couldn't find my boots."

Mr. P nodded. "I haven't bought my snow tires yet. Take a seat."

Dave slipped into his chair in the back row and buried his face in a novel.

Robbie looked over his shoulder and whispered, "Did you see Caesar's Facebook page today? He has a new profile picture."

"Nobody cares," Vanessa hissed. "Besides, it's quiet reading time."

Robbie looked over his other shoulder and asked Eric, "Did you leave a comment on

Caesar's video yet?"

Eric pretended not to hear. His head was bent over a poster he was colouring. It showed a rock band playing around a fir tree decorated with musical notes. *O Canada Holiday Fair*, it read. *Lord Nelson Gym. Friday, December 20th*.

"Caesar's going to be so excited when we get a Christmas tree," Robbie said to anyone who'd listen.

No one would listen.

"May I have your attention, please?" Mr. P announced. "I have some news about the Holiday Fair." He passed out a stack of green papers titled, "*The Lord Nelson Science Fair Needs Your Bright Ideas.*"

"There's a science fair in the gym on December 20th?" Taz asked.

"That's the day of the Holiday Fair," Dave said.

"And the location of the Holiday Fair," Eric added.

"Actually, it *is* the Holiday Fair," Mr. P said.

"I thought we were having music and a bake sale," Dave said.

"I may have given that impression," Mr. P admitted. "But it's actually a science fair."

"But you said the Nationals could play!" Dave complained. "We've been practising for weeks."

"I said I would *ask* if you could play," Mr. P clarified. "At which point, I was told that it's a science fair. So no."

"But I just finished the poster!" Eric whined. He held up his artwork.

"No whining," Mr. P said. "Remember the class rules." He pointed to a list on the front blackboard. It read: *No insults. No whining. No bullying. No pessimism. No lies.*

Taz raised his hand. "This announcement is dated a month ago."

"Yeah, that's a typo," Mr. P said. He rested his bottom on his desk and smiled. "Our theme for the science fair is 'Canada in the future.' I don't want to see any plaster volcanoes or silly experiments about what happens if you don't brush your teeth for a week. Those displays are boring. Been there, done that."

Taz raised his hand. "We're in grade six. We haven't been there. We haven't done that."

"But *I* have," Mr. P said. "And I want something more. Something exciting. Something that makes people think, 'Wow, that could really happen.'"

"Like a zombie apocalypse?" Nicolas asked. "Or an alien invasion?"

"Exactly!" Mr. P said. "Something science fiction-y. But . . . not."

Nicolas rubbed his hands together. "It's my time to shine."

Taz hung his head.

"Can I clone my dog?" Robbie asked.

"I doubt it," Mr. P said. "But you can try."

Dave raised his hand. "Can I perform the national anthem sung to the tune of 'O Christmas Tree'?"

Mr. P rolled his eyes. "That's not science."

"I could include a compass pointing north," Dave suggested.

"It has to be futuristic."

"What if we make our hearts actually glow?"

Mr. P ignored him.

Claire raised her hand. "Can I make a model of a dead planet floating through space?"

Everyone turned to her in surprise. She tucked her long, brown hair behind her ears and waited for an answer.

Mr. P frowned. "No pessimism, remember?"

Claire sighed. "It's a possible future."

At recess, Dave spotted Claire standing alone at the edge of the snowy soccer field. She was still looking glum. "You're not excited about the science fair?" he asked. "I thought you liked science."

She shrugged. "I don't like to think about the future. Global warming? Pollution? All the animals going extinct?" She shuddered.

Dave dragged his fingers on the ground and scooped up just enough snow to make a tiny snowball. "It sounds like you might have a phobia," he said, tossing the ball from hand to hand.

"Hah. Are you offering your fear-slayer services?"

"Maybe I could help." He shuffled from foot to foot and added, "It might take a while. We'd have to spend a lot of time together. Like maybe every day."

Claire braided the tassels of her scarf and shrugged. "Okay."

Dave blushed and nodded like a bobble-head doll. The future was looking good.

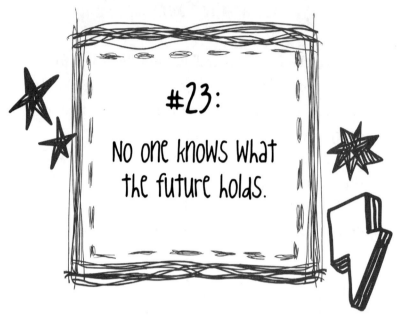

#23:

No one knows what the future holds.

"So what are you afraid of?" Dave asked Claire. They sat at his kitchen table, drinking hot chocolate and fidgeting. It was the first time they'd ever been alone together. "Nuclear war?" he suggested. "Terrorists? Epidemics? Toxic waste? Aliens?"

"All of those, I guess," Claire said. "Except aliens," she added. "I just can't think about the future. I don't know why."

"Sometimes it helps to break a big phobia into smaller bits," Dave said. "It's like cleaning your room. You know when your room gets so dirty that you have to wade through grubby clothes, old lunches, and overdue library books just to reach your bed?"

Claire made a face. "Why would I let my room get that messy?"

"You wouldn't," Dave said quickly. "Bad example. It's more like our reading journals. You know how Mr. P reminds us right before they're due? And then you think, 'Oh no, I forgot all about it and now I have to write four book reports this weekend?'"

Claire squinted. "Who would wait till the last minute to do all four reports?"

"Not me, that's for sure," Dave said. "No way. I'm totally on top of things, just like you. I've got everything under control." He sipped his hot chocolate and nodded in silence.

She pointed a finger at him. "You're a clever therapist, aren't you?"

Dave almost dropped his mug in surprise. "I am?"

She nodded. "You're getting me to answer my own questions. Right?"

Dave had no idea what she was talking about.

She put down her hot chocolate and smiled. "I like to have everything under control. I keep on top of things. So when I hear about bad stuff I can't control, I freeze. I feel helpless. I'd rather just not think about it."

"Yes," Dave said, nodding. "That's exactly what I hoped you would say."

She smiled. "So what do I do about it?"

Dave thought fast. "Ask yourself why you think bad stuff will happen. Maybe the future will be amazing. Maybe we'll have flying cars and robot servants and colonies on the moon."

Claire stared at him like he might be insane and she'd just never noticed before. "You'd have to be a fool to think that."

Dave's parents came home at that moment, followed by Nelson carrying a bucket of chicken. "Davy's got a girlfriend!" Nelson shouted when he saw Claire.

"I should be going," she said, rising quickly.

"Wait!" Dave said. "Let's get a second opinion." He turned to his father and asked, "Dad, what do you think the future holds?" Dave's father hung his gloves on the drying rack and sighed. "I worry sometimes that if the economy gets worse, people will cut back on dentistry and I'll lose the clinic."

"That's not the answer I was looking for," Dave said.

"Don't worry, dear," Dave's mother said, kicking off her boots. "If things get really bad, there'll be a lot more crime. So my job as a paralegal is secure."

Dave frowned. "You guys think the future will be awful?"

"No way! The future's going to be awesome," Nelson said. He waved a drumstick in the air as he described his vision. "There'll be flying cars and robot servants and colonies on the moon."

Claire looked at Dave and nodded as if she rested her case. "See you fools tomorrow."

At school the next morning, Mr. Papadakis led his class to the library to brainstorm "The Future." He sat at a table and pulled out his phone. "Take your time. Make it a brain hurricane."

Nicolas claimed a work table and asked, "Where's the alien section of the library?"

Taz folded his arms over his *Vote for Democracy* T-shirt. "This is my first science fair," he said. "I don't want to waste it on an alien invasion."

"Open your mind, Taz," Dave said. "Alien weapons, alien vehicles, alien communications, alien anatomy — there's tons of scientific potential."

"I'm interested in *human* life," Taz said.

Nic raised his palms. "So are the aliens!"

"I want to make a medical display," Taz said.

"Excellent," Dave said. "Let's say the aliens carry a deadly virus that threatens life on earth, and only experimental medicine can kill it."

"I could work with that," Taz admitted.

"Plus it makes our hearts glow," Dave added. He noticed Claire heading toward the nature shelves and said, "You guys take it from there. I'll try to recruit another group member."

He straightened his T-shirt and finger-combed his hair.

Then he sidled up to Claire and asked, "Want to join the alien invasion project?"

She shrugged. "I don't know. I might help Robbie clone Caesar."

"No! The world is already full of Shih Tzus."

She smiled. "I wanted to do animal parasites, but Mr. P said that's not futuristic."

"Our alien virus could be spread by parasites!" Dave tried to be cool and witty but he ended up babbling. "Parasites are cool. Have you ever had any? Maisy gets fleas sometimes. You want to be a vet, right? Vets are cool." He leaned against the bookshelf and knocked the entire pet section to the floor.

Claire helped him clean up his mess. She held up a book with a fluffy white terrier on its cover. "Maybe puppies are too cute for my vision of the future," she said. "Maybe I need an end-of-the-world situation like your group is doing. To face my fears, right?"

"Exactly," Dave said,

nodding happily. "You totally belong in our group. Our future is terrifying."

She smiled. "I'll think about it."

#24:

Life is full of surprises.

On Tuesday morning, Lord Nelson Elementary School's art teacher, Ms. Cuddy, waited at the front of Dave's classroom. "Mr. Papadakis had a family emergency, so I'll be taking over for a few days. He left this assignment." She handed out papers with the instruction, *Write a two-page report describing your role in Canada's future.* "Take ten minutes to discuss it."

Nicolas, Taz, and Andrew dragged their chairs to the back of the room. Eric took notes. Dave led the discussion. "So what do you think happened to Mr. P?"

"You're discussing your essays!" Ms. Cuddy shouted.

"So the aliens invade Earth," Dave said. "They drill into the planet, steal our resources, and infect us with a deadly virus spread by parasites."

"Why is it spread by parasites?" Eric asked.

"It just is," Dave said. "Who discovers the cure?"

"Me," Taz said, raising his hand. "I'll be the doctor. But I'm not dissecting any poor aliens." He shook his head and added, "I don't see why we have to fight them. Why can't we negotiate a truce?"

Nicolas shot him a glance like he was insane. "Because they're drilling into our planet, stealing our resources, and infecting us with a deadly virus! This is not the time for negotiation. We have to take these aliens down." He rubbed his hands together and smiled. "I'll handle the weapons."

"I'll sabotage the alien technology and break communications with their home planet," Eric said. "I'll be the computer genius."

"I don't know what I should do," Andrew said. "Science is not my strong subject. I don't see myself playing a big role in Canada's future except maybe on the stage."

"You could be a spy," Dave suggested. "That's kind of like acting. You could decode the alien language and infiltrate their ranks and pass secret information to our military."

Andrew nodded. "Would I get a costume with a glowing heart?"

"Sure. Why not?"

"How is that scientific?" Taz asked. He crossed his arms and huffed.

"Let's say the aliens are like giant bees," Dave said. "They communicate by dancing. Andrew will master their complicated dance language and lure them into a trap. He'll be a spy choreographer."

"Brilliant," Andrew said.

Taz did not look like he thought it was brilliant. "What's your role, Dave? You need to contribute something scientific."

Dave nodded. "I'll develop a musical therapy cure for all the terrified humans suffering from post-alien phobias."

Taz sunk his head in his hands.

Ms. Cuddy hovered in the aisle beside them, squinting. "This sounds more like drama than science."

"As an art teacher, you should encourage us to incorporate the arts into our assignments," Dave said.

She rolled her eyes. "Did you read the marking rubric?"

He read the marking rubric. "Fifty per cent of the grade is for research?" he exclaimed. "And we have to interview adults working in our field of study?"

Eric snorted. "Why would adults know anything about the future?"

"At least we're being marked on our individual contributions to the project," Taz muttered.

Claire walked over to Dave and asked, "Could I interview the vet who lives next door to you?"

"Yes," he said. "Any time. You bet. These interviews are a great idea."

"Thanks for letting me join your group," she told the boys.

They looked from her to Dave. "Claire's into parasites," he said.

"Cool. Yeah. Join the group," Andrew said.

"I'll interview the doctors at the clinic tonight," Taz said.

"I could email some tech professors," Eric said.

"I guess I could write a psychologist," Dave said.

"I'll go straight to the aliens," Nicolas said.

#25:

At any given moment around the world, something terrifying is happening.

Ms. Cuddy brought a stack of movies into class to fill her week of substitute teaching.

On Wednesday morning, they watched *The Itchy Earth*, about earthquakes, volcanoes, and landslides. Nicolas tapped Dave's shoulder. "What if there's a sinkhole under the school? We'd never get out alive."

In the afternoon, they watched *Wacky Weather*, about floods, droughts, and hurricanes. Taz passed Dave a note. *I'll be washed away before I get to become a doctor!*

On Thursday morning, they watched *Terrific Technology*, about nuclear weapons, toxic waste, and the looming terror of computer warfare.

"My life is online," Eric whined. "I'm toast."

In the afternoon, they watched *Bye-Bye Birdies*, about disappearing forests, global warming, and the spread of new fatal diseases. "What if Claire was psychic when she imagined a dead planet?" Andrew whispered.

Dave wondered how he could cure so many frightened friends. "I might start charging a fee," he announced.

By Friday morning, half the class was breaking Mr. P's "no pessimism" rule. "What's the point of going to school when we could die at any moment?" Nicolas sighed.

Dave rolled his eyes. "The chances of falling in a sinkhole are lower than being struck by lightning."

"One hundred lightning bolts hit the earth every second," Andrew said. "I'll probably be struck by lightning on my way home."

"At least you'll avoid the nuclear war set off by the next computer virus," Eric said.

"And you won't have to watch all the animals die in agony," Claire said.

"But you wouldn't have to do your science fair display," Taz added.

That perked everyone up a little.

"Come over after school today for group therapy," Dave said. "I might as well slay all your fears at once."

At 3:30, Claire, Nicolas, Taz, Andrew, and Eric gathered in Dave's basement. The boys crowded onto the couch while Claire sat in the armchair. Dave set two bowls of chips on the table and asked, "So, what are you all afraid of?"

Taz raised his hand. "My mom thinks a pig disease is going to mutate and infect humans and kill half the population of Earth."

"I talked to a guy who said computer warfare will wipe out everything we have," Eric said. "Economies will crash. Governments will fall. Criminal gangs will take over and sell us as slaves."

"I read that the polar ice caps are melting and the permafrost will thaw and release so much methane gas that the earth will get too hot to support life as we know it," Claire added.

"And before all that happens, I'll be swallowed by a sinkhole," Nicolas said.

"I can't sing the national anthem anymore,"

Andrew admitted. "Every time I say, 'I stand on guard,' I imagine tanks and hurricanes and killer bees charging me."

"Where do you get these worries?" Dave wondered. He flicked on the TV.

In the news, bombs tore apart a marketplace in the Middle East. Children cried for friends killed in a school shooting in the United States. Scientists discussed a deadly flu virus spreading through Asia. Doctors begged for money to save orphans starving in Africa.

Dave switched off the television. "I think your phobias might be caused by too much reality," he said. He turned to Nic and added, "Except yours. Yours might be caused by not enough reality."

He pushed the chip bowls aside to make room for his laptop compu-  ter. "Let's see what the experts recommend." He intended to search for group therapy advice, but he accidentally clicked his YouTube Favourites button, so they ended up watching videos of koala bears wrestling.

Everyone scrunched together in front of the screen. "They're adorable even when they're fighting to the death," Claire said.

The little round koalas hugged each other viciously.

Soon everyone was giggling and smiling and happily chatting.

Dave watched Claire's face light up as she watched the wildlife videos. "I think the first cure we should try is the Peter Pan treatment," he said.

"What's that?" Eric asked. "Fairy dust?"

"Close," Dave said. "Happy thoughts. Every time something scary comes to mind, just think happy thoughts. Distract yourself. Watch koala videos. Go Lego shopping. Pet a kitten. Don't think about what bothers you."

Claire frowned. "You mean pretend that everything's okay?"

"Everything *is* okay if you're watching cute animal videos," Dave said.

"I like it," Nicolas said. "It's pretty much the code I live by."

Dave smiled. "Avoid bad news. Increase good feelings. How could that be wrong?"

#26:
Ignore reality at your own risk.

A blizzard blew into town overnight and left so much snow that school was cancelled. Dave woke up, heard the news, and called Claire. "Our happy thoughts are paying off already!" he said. "Want to come over for therapy?"

"No thanks," she said. "I don't need therapy. I have happy thoughts. See you tomorrow."

Dave hung up. He felt a little sad so he made himself a strawberry smoothie. Nelson thumped downstairs and stole it right from his hand.

"Owned!" Nelson shouted, spouting a cloud of smelly morning breath. He smirked. "I think I'll call this a slave day instead of a snow day."

Dave scrounged for happy thoughts.

The next morning, Dave huddled in the snowy schoolyard with his friends. "So how's the Peter Pan treatment going?" he asked.

"Not so good," Eric said. "I didn't want to hear any bad news yesterday so I made my mom shut the radio off. Then I waited for the school bus for half an hour in the storm."

"I know," Nic said. "Vanessa posted a photo of you huddled at the bus stop with the caption, *Duh*. You looked really miserable."

"How'd the happy thoughts work for you, Nic?" Dave asked.

"Not so good," Nicolas admitted. "I wasn't happy thinking about clearing the table or emptying the dishwasher, so I didn't do those things. And now I get no allowance this week."

"I was scared of failing the French vocabulary test coming up this morning," Andrew said. "So I just didn't think about it. And now I'm pretty sure I'll fail since I didn't study."

Claire stomped through the yard toward them. "I wasted my whole snow day watching stupid YouTube videos and eating candy!" she complained. "When I started to feel bad about it, I went to the dollar store and blew all my money on junk. What a waste!"

Taz walked over smiling. "Hey, everyone! Wasn't the snow day wonderful?"

"Did you do the Peter Pan treatment?" Eric asked.

"No, it didn't feel right," Taz said. "I shovelled my neighbour's driveway for ten dollars. Then I finished my virus display."

Nic, Andrew, and Eric stared at Dave like it was his fault they weren't all done their homework and ten dollars richer.

Claire laughed. "You're such a great therapist, Dave."

He nearly fell down in surprise. "I am?"

She nodded. "I wouldn't have learned this lesson any other way."

"What lesson?" Eric asked.

Claire looked at each of the boys in turn. "Too much reality makes you depressed," she said. "But not enough reality makes you a fool. So what we need is just enough reality to manage. Right, Dave?"

"That was exactly the point I was making," Dave said, nodding. "Yup. That's right. A little fear can be a good thing."

Taz agreed. "Like you should all be a little more scared of what'll happen if you don't start working on our science display."

Dave nodded. "Let's look at the science fair as part of our therapy. We're imagining the worst possible future and learning how to kick its butt."

"Kicking butt always perks me up," Nicolas said.

On Saturday morning, the friends worked independently on their science fair displays.

Nicolas built an alien weapon that looked an awful lot like a Nerf gun.

Eric built an alien communications system that looked an awful lot like a hockey helmet with an iPod taped to it.

Andrew made a poster titled *AlienSpeak* that looked like tap dancing instructions.

Taz made a model of an infected human heart that actually looked like an infected human heart.

Dave made a three-panel display detailing the positive effects of music therapy on people suffering from stroke, Alzheimer's disease, depression, anxiety, and post-alien phobias. Then he emailed the prime minister with a request to write and perform a braver national anthem for Canada.

He was just about ready for some koala bear wrestling when Claire called. "I drew my parasite diagrams, but I need more ideas about how they might spread disease. Is your neighbour home?"

"Yeah. I'll ask him over," Dave said. "When can you get here?"

Dr. Walton drank an entire pot of tea while teaching Claire about his life's work. He spent half an hour describing the path of the rabies virus to a victim's brain, and another half an hour talking about all the pets he'd put to sleep after agonizing illnesses and injuries. "Then there was the dog that swallowed a pair of panty hose," he said. "They were all tangled up in his intestines."

Claire groaned. "I'm not sure I want to be a vet anymore."

"I remember every patient I ever had," Dr. Walton told her, smiling. "And I'm thankful for every one of them."

Claire bolted to attention. She turned to Dave with a smile. "You've done it again, haven't you?"

Dave knew better than to ask, Done what?

She slapped the table and shook her head. "I got sad sitting and listening to these gloomy stories. But Dr. Walton is happy thinking about them. Right?"

Dave thought she might be about to conclude that Dr. Walton was nuts, but instead she said, "That's because he didn't just sit around thinking about animals being sick, did he? No. He tried to make them better. And even if he couldn't save all of them, at least he tried."

"Exactly my point," Dave said. "Good work, Claire." He turned to Dr. Walton and said, "One last question, sir. How do you think veterinary medicine will change in the future? Do you think the rabies virus will mutate and turn pets into zombies?"

Dr. Walton frowned. "Not likely, son."

"Do you think scientists will create a dog-cat hybrid called doggats that'll guard us from burglars *and* mice?"

Dr. Walton shook his head. "No."

"Maybe there will be human-pet hybrids?" Dave suggested.

Claire smiled. "That could be an effect of the alien parasite," she said. "Maybe I can try to cure them."

Dave nodded. "And if they can't be cured, I can reduce their anxiety and depression with music therapy. Together we can help the little dog-dren and kid-dy cats."

Claire giggled. Dave held up his hand for a high-five.

"That's enough of the future for me," Dr. Walton said.

"Thanks for coming over, sir," Dave told him. He turned to Claire and asked, "Want to watch koala videos now?"

"Sounds good but I need to finish my display." She scooped up her notes with enthusiasm. "I love the idea of curing mutants. And I *do* want to be a veterinarian. Thanks, Dave. Maybe the future isn't so bleak, after all."

He smiled back, blushing. "Maybe what makes the difference is feeling like you can make a difference." He paused before saying, "I should put that on a T-shirt and give it to Taz."

#27:
There is always hope.

Dave was taping a final photograph of a human brain to his science display when the phone rang. It was Eric, and he was scared. "I looked up science fairs online," Eric said. "Our displays are lame compared to the ones that win scholarships."

"You need your reality dose adjusted," Dave said. "We're in grade six. We're not trying to win scholarships. We're trying to impress Mr. P."

"What if he's not back in time for the fair?"

"We should call him," Dave said. "Can you find out his number?"

"Sure. It's on his band's website."

Five minutes later, Eric had Mr. P on a conference call. "You're going to love our science display," Eric told him. "It's got biology, technology, and astrology."

"And musicology," Dave said. "Did you know that music doesn't just make you feel good, it actually helps repair the brain?"

"Sounds like you're learning a lot, boys," Mr. P said. "I can't wait to see it."

"How's the family emergency?" Dave asked.

"Fine. I had a baby."

"You had a baby?" Eric repeated. "We should have done our science display on you! We'd get scholarships for sure."

"My *wife* had a baby," Mr. P clarified. "She had to deliver early. Our daughter had something wrong with one of her heart valves. But she's had surgery and it looks like she'll be okay."

"Seriously?" Dave asked.

"Seriously," Mr. P said.

The boys were silent for a moment before Eric said, "You must have been scared."

Mr. P sighed. "Yup. But we're okay now. I'll see you at the science fair, boys. Make me proud."

The boys hung up and worked extra hard on their displays.

Half an hour later, Dave's phone rang again. "Are you the young man proposing a braver national anthem for Canada?" a strange voice asked. "I'd like to interview your band for a local good-news story."

"Yeah right," Dave said. "Nice try, Nelson." And he hung up.

On Thursday morning, Ms. Cuddy sent the class to the gym to set up their displays.

The alien invasion project took up twenty feet of wall space, including an assortment of graphs, charts, models, and diagrams, plus a twenty-two-inch television screen where Eric showed all the Nationals' videos spliced with footage from alien movies. "For people who don't care about the science stuff," he explained.

Taz frowned. "What if Mr. P hates it?"

"What if everyone thinks it's stupid?" Claire worried.

"What if we fail?" Andrew groaned.

"No pessimism, remember?" Dave said. "The human brain creates shortcuts for repeated thoughts and actions. So if you're always thinking, 'I'm afraid, I'm worried,' that idea gets carved into your brain. Just like the times tables."

"The times tables never got carved into my brain," Nicolas admitted.

"If someone's afraid, they shouldn't deny it," Taz said. "Happy thoughts got you into trouble, remember?"

"I'm not saying you should deny your fears. Just don't dwell on them," Dave said. "Instead of thinking about the one thing that could go wrong, think of all that could go right. Instead of thinking about the one thing you're scared of, think of all the things you're not scared of. Remember how awesome life really is. And how awesome we are." He smiled at each of his friends. "Like you, Taz. So you're afraid of infection. You're not afraid to stand up to bullies, are you?"

Taz smiled back proudly.

"Andrew, you're afraid of public speaking," Dave continued. "But you're not afraid to sing and dance in front of hundreds of people. And Eric, maybe you're afraid to look silly when you dance. But you show your drawings and movies to the whole world. And you, Nic, so you're afraid of sinkholes —"

"Actually, I'm over that," Nicolas said. "They're kind of a cool way to die."

Dave nodded. "Is there anything else you're afraid of?"

Nicolas shrugged. "Not that I know of."

"Okay, we'll skip you." Dave turned to Claire. "You say you're afraid of the future, Claire. But you're not afraid to find solutions or help animals or save mutants. And whatever the future holds, even if it's bad, there'll always be something you can save." He put his hands on his hips and added, "There'll always be a reason to be brave."

"There'll always be a new road you can pave," Eric added.

"You have the strength to swim against the wave," Nicolas said.

"Your fear will never make of you a slave," Taz cried.

"We have to write this down!" Andrew shouted. "It could be our new anthem!"

Claire laughed. "I love being in your group."

"You should join the band, too," Dave said. "Want to sing backup?"

After school, everyone met at Dave's house to record their new song of bravery. Andrew belted it out, wearing a flashlight under his T-shirt to simulate a glowing heart. Claire rapped in the background, calling upon Canadians to get busy building up democracy and wiping out hypocrisy.

"You rock," Dave told her.

"Let's post the video right now," Taz said.

Eric gasped. "Unedited?"

"Be brave," Nicolas told him.

"I'll send the prime minister the link," Dave said. "I've sent him all our videos so far. I really think he might be considering changing the anthem."

His friends exchanged glances. "There's always hope," Claire said.

#28:
Fear less.

On Friday morning, the Lord Nelson Elementary School gymnasium was crowded with posters and models and display panels, and noisy with conversation and laughter and Eric's artsy music videos. Mr. Papadakis walked through the doors and shouted, "You kids are blowing my mind!"

Dave's class flocked to their teacher, congratulating him and asking after his baby daughter. He showed them pictures on his phone. "We brought her home last night," he said. He looked up proudly and asked, "Why is Andrew wearing antennae?"

"This is my alien costume," Andrew said.

"Come see my bee dance."

Mr. P read through the entire alien invasion display. He learned about sonic weaponry, the human immune system, computer imaging, parasite biology, insect communication, and the effect of music on the brain. "I'm impressed," he said. "But why do you have your instruments on stage?"

"We're performing, of course," Dave said. "My subject is music therapy and this science fair is so depressing that everyone needs some."

"Did Principal Renault give you permission to play?" Mr. P asked.

The boys looked at each other. Their shoulders sagged.

Claire sighed. "Come on," she said. "Let's check out the other displays."

Nicolas nodded. "That'll cheer us up because ours is so much better."

A crowd hovered around Robbie's display table. It held a model DNA strand made from Smarties and a cardboard box containing Caesar and a toy chihuahua with its stuffing torn out.

"Problems with the cloning process?" Dave asked.

Robbie smiled. "Yeah. But Mr. P said my poster's excellent."

Next to him, Vanessa ran the *Virtual Travel Agency*. Her little sister Jessica sat in a lawn chair wearing a virtual reality headset that looked an awful lot like sunglasses taped to a pair of headphones. "I am loving my Disneyland vacation!" Jessica squealed.

Vanessa smiled. "Mr. P booked a trip to Costa Rica."

"Awesome," Claire said.

On the south side of the gym, among the grade eight displays, Nelson and Munster lounged on what appeared to be a garbage heap. They'd taped together grocery bags, water bottles, and toddler toys, and labelled it, *Crappenstuff: The New Continent*. Their display detailed how ocean currents were collecting humanity's garbage into a giant plastic island.

"I didn't know you cared about stuff like this," Dave told his brother.

"Do you propose any solutions to this terrible problem?" Taz asked.

"Are you kidding? I'm moving here," Nelson said, sipping from a plastic cup.

Dave nodded. "Works for me."

Principal Renault walked into the gym, followed by a man and a woman wearing suits and carrying black cases. They walked straight up to Dave.

"I'm sorry about the copyright infringement!" Eric shouted.

"Are you Dave Davidson from the Nationals?" the man asked.

"These are reporters from KTTV," Principal Renault explained. "They're doing a story on the Holiday Fair."

The woman took a camera from her case. The man stepped in front of it and spoke into a microphone. "I'm here with staff and students at the Lord Nelson Elementary School Holiday Fair. And let me assure you, there's some visionary work on display here today."

Mr. Papadakis looked around the room, slightly confused.

"I'm looking at a fascinating display created by a student band called the Nationals," the reporter continued. "But it's their comedic

videos of the national anthem that have really caught our ear."

"Comedic videos?" Eric repeated, frowning.

The reporter nodded. "We'd like to put one of your anthems on the six o'clock news."

"I think we just got our permission to perform," Dave whispered to Mr. P.

The reporter smiled. "I'm sure the prime minister is pleased to know your version of a powerful national anthem is out there inspiring other young Canadians. I call your latest song, 'O Can-do Canada.' I think the whole country would be entertained by it."

Andrew jumped up and down. "The whole country will be singing our song!"

"We're going to get so many YouTube hits," Eric said.

"We'll be famous!" Nicolas shouted.

"We're getting an A for sure," Taz said.

"'O Can-do Canada'," Dave muttered. "Why didn't we think of that?"

The reporter interviewed Mr. P and all his students. "Will we really be on TV tonight?" Vanessa asked excitedly. Robbie picked up Caesar and mugged for the camera.

Eric, Nicolas, Taz, Andrew, and Claire told the story of how they discovered their artistic genius, their love of country, and their cure for an alien virus.

"You kids aren't scared of anything," the reporter said. He turned to the camera and smiled. "Let's close with a few words from the boy behind the petition for a new anthem."

The camera zoomed in on Dave. For a moment, his mind went blank with terror. Then Eric nudged him, and he shifted into speech mode.

"Every fear is a fear of the future," Dave said. "It's the fear that something terrible is about to happen and you won't be able to handle it. But when we waste our time being scared of stuff that's probably never going to happen, then we don't spend enough time helping each other get through the stuff that actually *is* happening." He pointed a finger at the camera and smiled. "So be brave. Make the world *less* scary. Help somebody feel *better* about the future."

"This kid should go into politics," Principal Renault whispered.

"It would be a better choice than science," Mr. P agreed. "How about a song from the Nationals?" he shouted.

The kids climbed onto the stage. Claire squeezed Dave's hand and whispered, "I've never performed in public before. I'm scared."

"You'll be great," Dave told her. "You *are* great. But I need that hand to play guitar."

She let go with a smile.

They played "O Can-do Canada" and "O Canada Christmas Tree," and the audience asked for an encore. Dave stepped up to the microphone and introduced the band. "That's Taz Santos on keyboards, Nicolas Talwar on drums,

Andrew McFadden on vocals and ukulele, Claire Leblanc on backup vocals, and over there is   Eric Leung, our manager, sound tech, and videographer. And I'm Dave Davidson. We're the Nationals! We're the future! And the future is fearless."

Also by Catherine Austen

26 Tips for Surviving Grade 6

Forget social studies, math, and science — this hilarious novel is about surviving some of the real problems tween girls face in the sixth grade. Honest and heartwarming, the story follows eleven-year-old Becky Lennox over the course of the school year as she figures out how to survive friendships, first crushes, embarrassing parents, and annoying older brothers.

Hackmatack Children's Choice Book Award, 2013

Quebec Writers' Federation Prize for Children's and Young Adult Literature, 2012

"Delightful and spot-on for the middle grade experience . . . what a fun choice for a mother-daughter book club.

Laugh-out-loud funny and great opportunities for moms to share their own sixth grade experiences as they flood back after reading this."

— *Deb Marshall, Just Deb*
http://mylibrarynotebook.blogspot.ca

". . . a simply told yet fast-paced and colourful blend of humour and drama . . . well-rounded, credible characters . . . This book will certainly appeal to female readers. Highly Recommended."

— *CM: Canadian Review of Materials*